Chapter One

E VEN WITH THE anxiety over her first day of work at her new job looming, Lexie Parker still took the time to count out the brightly colored pills and filled the plastic holder, labeled by individual days and divided by a.m. and p.m. doses. She separated each medication and double-checked the dose on the list provided to her by her sister's doctor. In a separate pill holder, she included a daily dose of antianxiety medication, also doctor-prescribed and approved.

She clicked each holder shut tight, then left the plastic containers next to the cookie jar in the kitchen for her sister, along with ten dollars for coffee and breakfast downstairs at the market on the corner. Any extra change would probably be hoarded for shopping, but she'd accepted that particular vice. As long as she could keep Kendall on her meds, Lexie could breathe more easily. Her sister might not appreciate the effort, but Lexie knew, if not for her, the psych ward was waiting. Again.

Her sister's dog, Waffles, a small terrier mix she'd adopted during one of her manic phases, jumped up and down, begging for a treat.

"No. You just had breakfast, you piggy," Lexie said, bending to pat the tan fluffy dog on the head. "You're on a diet." Her sister tended to overfeed him, when she remembered to feed him at all.

Lexie ticked off her list of morning chores, satisfied she'd remembered everything before sparing a glance at the second bedroom in her apartment—paid for with her father's money. His way of showing gratitude for her sacrifice. She'd lost her last job because she'd been too busy looking after Kendall during her last depressive episode. The one that had landed her in Shady Oaks.

Lexie hated accepting her parents' money, but she'd been unemployed and out of options, and they'd leased this apartment for them a few months ago. After her sister's doctor had agreed to release her following a two-week stay in the psych ward, as long as she lived with someone who could keep an eye on her. Though her parents had a huge home on Long Island, Lexie had taken the burden off of them and agreed to the new living arrangement.

After all, Kendall was her twin. And her father had

his hands full with her mother, who suffered from severe depression. Yes, her family had fantastic genes. Lexie always feared she was one bad mood away from falling prey to the same demons that consumed her mother and sister.

Lexie rushed into her room to get ready for her first day at her new job. The position wasn't glamorous. She'd been hired on as a personal assistant to a software mogul whose company her father was investing in. Her employment was a favor, since she didn't have a glowing letter of recommendation from her last job.

Her dreams of working in a PR agency in Manhattan had disappeared when she transferred to a local college not long after her sister had returned home following her first breakdown. Lexie had taken classes and finished her degree but wasn't able to build a career that lasted. Life was always busy, and her twin's periods of stability weren't long enough.

Despite her busy morning routine, Lexie couldn't afford to be late. She'd read the online write-ups on Kaden Barnes, software billionaire whose company was giving Snapchat a run for the money. Kaden was the financial guru behind the business, and if his partners were to be believed, he couldn't keep a personal assistant because he was too difficult to work for.

She wasn't worried ... much. The one thing Lexie was good at was keeping other people organized and ignoring frustrating personalities. She was sure she could deal with the stuffy billionaire with a stick up his ass.

She dressed in her best skirt and blouse, chose a pair of heels she could walk in without too much pain, picked up her purse, and started for the door.

"Lexie!" Kendall called, yanking her door open and rushing into the room. "I had the best idea for a job. What if I board dogs?" she asked, scooping Waffles into her arms. "You want playmates, don't you?" she asked, nuzzling the pup's fur.

Drawing a deep breath, Lexie turned. "We aren't allowed more than one pet in this building, so I'm afraid you'll have to keep thinking. I have to get to work, so we'll talk later. Your meds are on the counter and so is money for lunch."

"God dammit, you're not my mother. I'm twenty-eight years old! I don't need a babysitter," she exploded. She bent and placed the dog on the floor, then glared at Lexie.

No, the meds hadn't calibrated correctly yet, she thought, trying her best to maintain her composure. When Kendall was level-headed, she appreciated Lexie's efforts at helping.

Ignoring her outburst, otherwise she'd end up engaged in a full-on war of words, which was what her sister wanted, she waved good-bye. "See you later!" she said and rushed out the door.

Unfortunately, when she reached the ground level and exit and opened the door to the street, rain sprinkled down just as the bus she planned on taking pulled up to the corner.

There was no time to run back upstairs for an umbrella, so she braved the rain and hoped she didn't look like a drowned rat by the time she arrived at her new job.

KADEN BARNES WALKED out of yet another unproductive settlement meeting, his business partners, Derek West and Lucas Monroe, by his side. He exited into an early-morning drizzle. From the wet look of the ground, the skies had opened up while they were indoors, and his foot hit a puddle before he climbed into the waiting Town Car.

Fucking swell. This day was just fantastic already, and it was barely nine a.m. Julian Dane, their former friend, was suing them for a piece of their company and a huge chunk of money. Today's plan had been to set the meeting early, intending to catch him at a weak moment, when he wouldn't be as focused and ready to talk terms. The bastard trying to steal a piece of their empire had a problem with partying and a bigger issue with drugs. As they all knew from experience, mornings were rough on him.

Unfortunately, all the power plays in the world didn't matter. According to their attorney, because Julian had been there during the initial design phase, they'd have to come up with some kind of settlement if they wanted this mess to go away. In Kade's book, any acknowledgment of Julian's supposed hand in the creation of the Blink app was a loss. And Kade didn't like to lose.

He remained silent on the ride downtown to their Soho offices while Derek and Lucas talked about potential offers Julian might accept. Kade was still brewing on that. The man had a cocaine problem. Money would probably be the most welcome solution. Lord knew he hadn't been interested in rehab when offered, and no way in hell would they give him a stake in the company.

"You could have shaved for this meeting," Derek said as they exited the car a little while later.

Lucas slammed the door behind them and laughed. The asshole.

Kade shrugged. "I wore a suit. You can't have everything."

They'd agreed to dress like the adults they were, not the tee-shirt-wearing juveniles they preferred to be, in order to let Julian know he wouldn't be walking all over them. They were taking his lawsuit seriously—because if it dragged out and ended up in court, their company valuation would be impacted. They couldn't afford to let that happen, and Julian knew it. Which meant he had the upper hand.

Still stewing over that fact, Kade followed the others into the elevator. He hit the button for the top floor, heading up to the area above the workspace they shared with employees. The offices were housed in a newly renovated garage.

He strode past the abstract paintings surrounded by steel beams toward his private office and stepped inside. The wall-to-wall windows provided him with a full view of the gloomy rain that matched his mood. All he wanted was to hole up at his desk and work on the funding. No distractions, no bothersome annoyances, no—

"Good morning, Mr. Barnes," a chipper voice said, popping up from beneath his desk.

He blinked in surprise, then narrowed his gaze at the strange woman he'd never seen before. "Who the hell are you, and what are you doing under there?"

"I moved your computer and was plugging it back in," she said, pointing to the far corner of his desk. "You can pull it forward when you need to work. I set the keyboard at a better ergonomic location so it's safer for your back. Not to mention, you'll have easier access to your files when you're sitting at your desk," she explained, clasping her hands in front of her.

His lips firmed, and he was about to rip into her when he realized she looked as if she'd been caught in the morning's downpour. Her brown hair was damp, curling at the ends, and her white shirt had water stains on the front, calling attention to a lace bra and her full breasts. None of which detracted from the beauty beneath the smudged makeup. With big blue eyes and porcelain skin, she was exactly Kade's type.

Not skinny and more than a handful, he thought, his mouth watering at the thought. "And my other question? Who are you?" he asked, his voice harsh in order to cover the sudden rush of desire he didn't need riding him here and now.

"Lexie Parker, your new personal assistant," she said, her voice soft and pleasing, at distinct odds with her bossy personality, if her nerve in rearranging his desk before meeting him was anything to go by. His anxiety and ADHD were off the charts with a mere glance at the new setup, not that he'd admit to such a thing.

When he remained silent, she placed her hand on the stapler—on his now neat desk. Folders sat in precise stacks; his favorite pen was nowhere to be found, probably mixed in with the writing utensils in the holder he never used. His organized disorganization was gone. Not even his meds took the edge off her changes.

"I didn't hire you," he said through gritted teeth.

"I see you two have met," Derek said, joining them in his office and slapping Kade on the back as he drew up beside him. "Think you can hold on to this one?"

Kade unclenched his jaw. "Did I miss the interview?" he asked.

"Lexie is Wade Parker's daughter," Derek said, naming their biggest backer and investor. "She needed a job, and you, my friend, need a personal assistant you can't run off with your not-so-charming personality and demands."

His eyes shot daggers at his partner, who knew full well he liked to choose his own PA, before glancing back at Lexie. She smiled and treated him to a small wave. His dick responded to her smile. The wave irritated the shit out of him.

He turned to face her. "Guess we're stuck with each other."

She smiled, and it brightened her entire face, lighting up incredibly blue eyes. Sky blue, his favorite color. "So what next?" she asked.

"Don't touch my stuff without permission."

She frowned, her eyes narrowing, drawing attention to her dark lashes. "How about you try my changes. If you don't like them, I'll put things back the way I found them." She patted his chair, indicating he should sit.

Well, what do you know? She wasn't intimidated by him.

He met her gaze and grinned, extending his hand. "Just ask before you touch my things next time."

"Yes ... sir." They shook hands, and the feel of her soft flesh sent waves of desire rippling along his skin. He jerked his hand back quickly.

Derek chuckled. "I think you two will get along just fine." He leaned in close and whispered in Kade's ear. "And since she's Wade's daughter, you can trust her with your keys. You won't have to pick up your own dry cleaning." Another slap on the back, and he walked out the door.

"Would you like to make a list of what's expected of me?" Lexie asked eagerly.

He groaned. A peppy, sexy personal assistant wasn't what he'd had in mind. Of course, he'd run off the older woman before Lexie (too many personal errands for her taste), the young woman right out of college (she'd come on to him and looked like jailbait, and when he'd not-so-politely turned her down, she'd walked out on the spot), and another PA who hadn't appreciated his request for coffee every morning. She'd said it went against her feminist sensibilities.

He'd told her he didn't give a shit and she'd quit.

Lucas claimed Kade had control and trust issues with women and drove them off on purpose. He was right about one thing. Kade didn't trust most females. The first one in his life had abandoned him by choice, and the ones who'd come after had betrayed him. That didn't just jade a man. It embedded an ugly truth deep in his psyche. Women either wanted something or would stab him in the back, one way or another.

His personal assistant, as much as he needed one, had the potential to get too close and intimately involved, at least in his private life. Add in the fact that the woman waiting for his instructions was beautiful, and things were destined to get complicated. But he needed the help, something Derek obviously knew. So Lexie Parker was his, at least for now.

"Let's start with you giving my desk back."

He cocked an eyebrow and waited for her to walk around the piece of furniture, providing a view of nice legs beneath her pencil skirt that ended just above the knee and an ass she knew how to sway as she walked. With the way his body tightened, her damned hem might as well hit mid-thigh.

Pissed at himself, he strode around her, catching a whiff of a warm, feminine scent he couldn't name but would never forget.

"I'll just go get a pen and paper," she said.

"Here." He handed her a yellow lined notepad and a pen, pulled from the holder she'd moved to the right side of his desk.

He gestured for her to sit before easing himself into his luxurious leather chair and tipping back, getting as comfortable as he could within the confines of his suit. He much preferred his well-worn jeans. He loosened his tie and undid the top button of his dress shirt, his gaze locking with hers. She'd been staring, watching his every move.

Caught, her cheeks flushed a pretty pink, and she ducked her head, busied herself, making a show of clicking the pen open and getting ready to take notes.

He steepled his fingers and began to rattle off his list of daily needs. "First things first. Coffee waiting for me at nine. I like it fresh, hot, black with three sugars. You'll keep my schedule of meetings. I tend to forget without a reminder. You'll accompany me to meetings, get a feel for this business and anything I'm currently working on. I need you fluent in tech." He glanced over his fingers to find her writing quickly.

Finishing up, she met his gaze. "Ready."

Here's where the issues and deal breakers usually came in. "I'll expect you to pick up my dry cleaning from my house on Tuesdays and Saturdays and drop it off at my apartment." He handed her a card from his top desk drawer. "My preferred dry cleaner's address."

He spared her another look as she merely accepted the card. She didn't balk at doing his personal chores. Surprising respect rose before he smothered it.

"Got it. What else?" she asked.

Undeterred, he continued. "I work from home often. On those days I'll ask you to bring me lunch or work from there as well."

She nodded once again.

"No complaints so far?"

An amused smile lifted the corners of her mouth. "Nope. You haven't run me off yet. So what do you like to eat for lunch?"

"Grilled chicken on whole wheat bread, mayonnaise, and two slices of avocado. There's a place downstairs that delivers." He slid another business card across the desk.

She picked it up, drawing his attention to her pink fingernails. Delicate, long fingers, made for curling around his—

"Keys. I'll need a key to your house," she said, interrupting his inappropriate train of thought.

"Apartment," he muttered, annoyed she was a step ahead of him. And also irked by the fact that he couldn't stop thinking about her in a sexual way. It was going to make working with her damned distracting. "I'll get you a key soon." He always had his locks changed after a PA didn't work out.

"Is there anything else?" she asked, sliding the pen along her lip in a gesture surely not meant to be erotic, but his body registered it that way nevertheless.

"No. You can go home," he snapped.

"Excuse me?" she asked, eyes wide. "You can't just fire me for no good cause."

"I didn't. I'm giving you a break. You can't be comfortable in that damp shirt," he said, deliberately letting his gaze trail over the water stains on her chest.

Those luscious lips opened, then closed again in horrified shock.

Go ahead, sweetheart. Call me on sexual harassment, he thought. At least that would end his pain. He couldn't spend another minute wondering what color her nipples were beneath that lacy bra, and his jaw hurt from clenching his teeth so hard.

When she remained silent, he knew she was stronger than he'd given her credit for. "I'm going to work from home this afternoon," he told her, making the spur-of-the-moment decision. "Leave me your email and cell number, and I'll send you a grocery list. You can fill it and bring it by later today. My fridge is empty."

Realizing he'd have to have a company credit card put in her name if she worked out, he rose and reached into his pocket for cash, handing her money to pay.

"I need your address," she reminded him.

He picked up yet another business card, *his*, and handed it to her. "I'm uptown. Keep track of mileage, bus or subway fares, and you can submit expense reports."

"Yes ... Boss." She rose and hugged the clipboard to her chest. "You'll be happy with me," she promised him. "You'll see."

Oh, he was plenty happy with her. He was more curious how long she'd be happy with *him* and his endless demands.

Chapter Two

LEXIE DIDN'T KNOW how she'd held it together in front of Kaden Barnes. She'd been expecting a geeky nerd with a Napoleon complex who'd changed the face of social media. Instead she'd gotten a hot, arrogant, sexy-as-sin, pain-in-the-ass, panty-melting boss. And he'd seen through her, literally, in her damp, see-through blouse. No way had the man been impressed with her in any way. Great way to begin her new job, she thought, her mood sinking even further.

She let herself into her apartment to find her sister wasn't home and she'd taken Waffles with her. She headed straight for the bedroom. She changed into a new blouse, freshened her makeup, and pulled her straggly hair up into a bun. The best she could do given the circumstances. It was still humid outside after the rain passed, and she didn't want to leave her hairstyle up to the elements.

She knew Kendall wouldn't expect her back midday, so she decided to do a spot check on her meds and make sure she'd been taking them. Or at least pretending to take them. The most she could hope for was that today's pills were gone from the container. Whether her sister took them or flushed them, time would tell. She hoped for the best but expected the worst. The doctors said people with bipolar disorder often had multiple hospitalizations before coming to terms with the illness and beginning to take their meds on a regular basis.

She looked in the kitchen, where she'd left the pills along with a note, but the counter was empty. With guilt but also a sense of resignation, Lexie knocked once to be safe and opened the door to her sister's bedroom, planning to do a quick visual sweep of the counters. Her gaze immediately went to department store shopping bags on the floor, and it felt like her stomach plummeted.

Compulsive shopping usually happened on one of her sister's manic episodes. Lexie sighed, wondering where she'd gotten the money. She didn't have credit cards of her own thanks to the last time she'd abused the privilege and their father had to bail her out. She hoped Kendall hadn't talked either parent into giving her money or a credit card behind Lexie's back. Both her mother and father found it hard to say no to

Kendall when she asked nicely and made excuses that were too easy to believe for why she needed something.

Lexie didn't have time to dwell on it now. She glanced at the nightstand and saw the medicine holder, with today's pills gone from the container. Well, maybe something was going right. She'd just have to deal with the shopping issue another time. She stepped out and shut the door behind her.

She gathered her things, made sure she had the email on her phone, and headed to food shop for her boss. As she went up and down the aisles of her local grocery store, she discovered he was a heath nut with a sweet tooth, from his coffee to the four large packages of Twizzlers red licorice on the list.

She wondered what his dental bills were like. Which led her to think of his gorgeous smile, which he didn't use often. In fact, she thought she might have seen it once in their first meeting, when he'd realized she wouldn't let him push her around.

She grinned at the memory and finished up her list, then paid for the items with the money he'd given her. A bagger asked to help her outside while she hailed a cab, and she gratefully took him up on the offer.

A little while later, she arrived at his luxury building. A doorman met her. She gave her name; he greeted her with a friendly smile and a nod and pulled out a cart, proceeding to transfer the bags while she paid the driver.

Every so often, worry over the shopping bags she'd found in her sister's room and the fact that Kendall hadn't been home surfaced, but Lexie pushed the concerns aside. She'd have to compartmentalize if she wanted to succeed at this job, and she did. Badly.

Despite the part of her nature that needed to be a caretaker, she also wanted to earn her own way and succeed in whatever employment she chose. Not only wouldn't she let Kaden Barnes drive her off with his demands, she wouldn't allow her family issues to intrude on her professional life.

Her personal problems already prevented her from having a private life, and she'd lost so much by putting Kendall before everyone and everything else. She couldn't allow her sacrifices to keep extending into all areas. She'd keep this job if it killed her, she thought, and worry about things like dating and sex when her sister turned a corner.

"Go on up. I'll bring these up the service elevator," the doorman said. "Penthouse."

Of course, she thought. No regular floor for Kaden Barnes. She took the elevator up and stepped out into a well-lit hallway with only one apartment door to be found.

She rang the bell. Nobody answered. She rang

again. If he'd stayed at the office and forgotten to tell her, she'd… Before she could finish that thought, the door swung open wide, and he stood before her, wearing nothing but a towel tucked around his waist in all his bare-chested glory.

Her gaze traveled from his dark brown hair, handsome face—he hadn't bothered to shave—down his chest, taking in the sleeve of tattoos on one arm, giving him an even sexier edge. Finally her gaze dropped to the towel knotted at his hip, and she sucked in much-needed air. Her girl parts definitely took notice, and considering it had been a *long* time since she'd been with any man, she was definitely aware of the rush of desire sweeping through her body and the sudden tingling between her thighs.

"Did you forget I was *coming?*" she asked, her voice catching on that last word, which she hadn't meant as a sexual innuendo but felt like one anyway.

"No, that's not something I could forget." Amusement and a rough timbre laced his tone, letting her know he'd picked up on it too.

Her cheeks burned. "Your doorman should be up with the food any minute. Am I expected to put it away too?" she asked, deciding it was best to move past her foot-in-mouth moment.

"The housekeeper will do it. She's here today."

"Okay then. I can just go back to the office and—"

He reached out and grasped her arm, generating a jolt of heat that ricocheted through her.

He jerked and immediately released her. "Come in and get familiar with the place. You'll be working here," he said gruffly.

He stepped back to let her inside, shutting the door behind her. "I'll go get dressed. Keep yourself busy," he muttered and stalked off, leaving her alone to examine his home.

She shrugged and began walking through the apartment, which was huge, with state-of-the-art everything. The kitchen, which she passed on the way to a big living area, had high-end appliances, from a Wolf oven and Sub-Zero refrigerator to a Miele dishwasher. She doubted he used any of them himself. Still, she was in *love* with his kitchen.

And the living room? Of course there was a massive screen on the wall and a full tech setup of Xbox and Wii devices for the geek in him. She loved it and could very well imagine him sitting here, playing his games, and envisioning life-changing apps.

The room itself resembled a cinema, and she sat down on an oversized sofa, sinking into the soft leather. She didn't go so far as to extend the chair into a reclining position, choosing to remain upright and keep her wits about her. While she waited, she looked around, and her gaze fell to a set of photos on wall shelves across the room.

Intrigued, she rose and walked over, taking in the various photographs. There were pictures of Kade and his partners wearing frat shirts from their college days. Some of Kade and an older man who was obviously, based on the resemblance, his father. And in the back row, a small shot of two young boys who appeared about the same age and who looked remarkably alike.

Being a twin herself, Lexie was curious and picked up the small picture. She thought she could pick out Kaden. He was a little taller and bulkier. Both brown-haired boys stood in mimicking poses with their arms crossed over their chests, both in bathing trunks, with a pool behind them, and mischievous smirks on their faces.

"What do you think you're doing?"

She jumped, very much feeling like she'd been caught snooping. Which, she supposed, in theory, she had been.

"You said to keep myself busy." She handed him the photograph. "Is that your twin?" she asked.

"My brother." He glanced at the picture in his hand, and she caught a wistful expression before he hid it with his normal outward mask of indifference.

"Older or younger?" she asked, undeterred. If she was going to work with him, she needed to break through his barrier and at least get him to converse with her.

"Younger. By only ten months."

She grinned. "Your parents worked fast."

"That's what happens when you spend more time arguing and making up than getting along," he muttered.

Insight, she thought, appreciating the nugget of information.

"I thought you were here to work." He set the picture in its spot in the back row.

Something told her the placement of the photo was telling. A story she wanted to know more about, but he wasn't talking.

Yet. "You told me to wait for you while you dressed. You're dressed."

And if she thought she'd seen all facets of Kaden Barnes, from the man in the suit to the fresh-from-the-shower version, she was wrong. This man, in the gray sweat pants that hung low on his hips and faded white tee shirt that read *Geek Squad* across his chest—she had a hunch this was the real man beneath the façade he put out to the world.

Despite his gruff exterior, his sex appeal couldn't be denied, and the little hint of vulnerability she'd seen when he'd looked at the picture of his brother made him seem even more human.

Sensing she'd pushed him out of his comfort zone

enough for one day, she turned her focus to work. "So what's next … Boss?"

He studied her for a few seconds, then said, "Call me Kade. And give me your phone."

"What?"

"Your cell phone." He held out his hand.

She dug through her purse and reluctantly handed over her iPhone.

"Unlock it."

She glared at him.

"Please," he added.

"That's much better." She took back the phone and opened it with her fingerprint before returning the device. "I can't imagine what you want—"

He slid his finger over the screen, checking out each display of apps before moving to the next screen. Suddenly realizing what he was looking for, she braced herself for the reprimand.

"You don't have Blink on your phone. How can you possibly work for me if you don't have the app and know what it's all about?"

KADE EYED HIS personal assistant with frustration, which was a helpful emotion, serving to tamp down on the desire that had been riding him since he'd opened his door and seen her gaze raking over him appreciatively. She'd changed her top, and though her work outfits were completely appropriate, his imagination went into overdrive thanks to the fancy buttons holding her shirt closed over her full breasts and the same skirt from earlier, which accentuated her rounded hips.

He was annoyed that he'd caught her with his photographs and pressing for information about his family. Information that dug at him like an open wound.

He hadn't seen Jeffrey in over twenty years, their parents' ugly divorce and subsequent division of custody making sure the adults—and boys who were as close as could be—ended up living on different continents. With one stroke of the pen, Kade had lost the mother who'd given birth to him and his best friend.

Looking back, his mother hadn't been such a loss. She'd always favored Jeffrey, *the easier child*, while Kade, with his colic, undiagnosed learning disabilities, which he now knew were ADHD and anxiety, had been challenging from birth. Not to mention what he thought was mild OCD. All of which his mother had never let him forget, and which had provided a lesson he'd taken into adulthood with his relationships.

He'd had difficulties in school, problems making friends, and his mother had no patience or desire to find out *why*. She called him stupid and annoying, a pain, saving her affection for Jeffrey. Yet somehow, Kade hadn't resented his younger brother. He'd looked up to him for being all the things Kade couldn't manage to be.

And one day he was gone. Madeline Barnes had taken off, choosing to move far away and cut off contact rather than share custody. Kade hadn't been good enough for his own mother. He was never quite good enough. His difficulties had followed him into adulthood, and he didn't think any woman would put up with him for long. And the ones in his life hadn't. They'd grown impatient with his quirks; some were embarrassed, causing him to pull further into himself.

He shook his head, forcing himself back to the present. He didn't appreciate the unpleasant memories Lexie had dredged up, but instead of true anger, he found himself surprised she'd been interested. When most people wouldn't have looked that closely at pictures of his childhood or wondered anything about him beyond his bank account, she'd seemed honestly curious.

And he wondered about her in return. He wasn't a typically social person, and his inquisitiveness about her made him uncomfortable. He needed to put a wall back between them and fast. Which was why he held Lexie's cell phone in his hand, searching for his pride and joy, only to find his app was nowhere to be found.

He stared at her, waiting for an explanation to his question.

"I-I'm not big on social media," she stammered, the first sign that he'd rattled her. "But you're right. It was a stupid oversight, and I'll correct it right now." She grasped back her phone, and with trembling hands, she hit the button for the app store and downloaded Blink in seconds.

He waited in silence as she opened it and created an account. "I'll be sure to learn it later today."

"Good idea." He gestured for her to sit down, and she lowered herself into one of the sections of the sofa. He loved the oversized white leather and the electric recliners in each part. Not to mention the built-in fridge where he kept Smartwater and vitamin drinks.

She fidgeted in her seat. He couldn't tear his gaze from her long legs that he could envision up in the air, settled on his shoulders, as he lowered his head to her sweet pussy. "Shit."

"What's wrong?" she asked.

He hadn't meant to speak out loud. "Not a damned thing. I thought maybe we could see how you perform in my world." He picked up a remote and spoke. "Television on." The ninety-inch flat-screen on the wall flickered to life. "Mario Party," he said, reveling in the surprise on her face as he loaded his Wii U.

"You want us to play video games?" Her blue eyes opened wide.

"I do."

"Mario? Seriously?" she asked, clearly not convinced.

"Yes."

She studied his face as if she didn't believe him or was waiting for him to crack a smile. She'd have to wait all night, and he was damned patient. When she didn't reply, he handed her a controller and picked up one of his own.

"You *are* serious. Did you make all of your other PAs go through this ... test?"

"No."

"Why not?"

Because he didn't care if his other PAs could hold their own with him. She'd already proven she wasn't intimidated by him, a point in her favor. "Consider yourself special."

In the span of the one hour total he'd spent in her company, he'd realized he wanted to see what made her tick. She didn't seem to fear him, and he liked that about her. He had a hunch he could enjoy her company—if he let himself. Not to mention, his cock really liked having her around, and it'd been a damned long time since he'd had sex.

Too long. Because he didn't trust women to get close. Lexie was already there.

Pushing that thought aside, he offered her a soda, which she declined.

"Do you need instructions?" he asked, assuming video games were foreign to her as they'd been to most women he'd dated.

She wrinkled her nose in thought. "Nope. I think I can handle it."

He blinked, startled. Not even Angela, the one woman he'd thought he was in love with, when he'd been young, hormone-driven, and stupid enough to forget the lessons his mother had taught him, had had patience for his *childlike games*. She'd had plenty of interest in his *things*. And now he referred to her as the bitch who'd betrayed him.

He glanced at Lexie, who studied the screen, sucking her bottom lip between her teeth, and wondered what it was about her that brought up things about his past he tried to keep buried. Once again, he pushed those thoughts aside.

And for the next few hours, she impressed him once more, immersing herself in the game. He found her to be competitive, like him. Creative in her thinking, like him. And she was a damned good strategist. Also like him.

And to top it all off, she really got into the game, allowing herself to have fun. She'd long since kicked off her shoes and curled her legs beneath her on the sofa. Her hair fell out of the bun, long strands curling around her shoulders. Her blue eyes flashed with enjoyment and determination, and damned if, by the end of the day, he didn't *like* her.

Finally, he dropped the controller, and she did the same, flinging herself back against the sofa with a wide grin on her face. "I think I rocked it, don't you?" she asked, obviously pleased with herself.

He casually lifted one shoulder. "You held your own." A smirk lifted the corner of his mouth, and she burst out laughing.

"I almost kicked your ass!" she squealed, then sobered quickly. "I'm sorry. With all the game playing, I forgot you were my boss."

The light flickered out of her gaze, and he missed the warmth she'd exuded earlier. "It's fine."

She shook her head. "No." She rose to her feet, smoothing the wrinkles out of her skirt.

"Lexie," he said in a controlled tone, pulling her out of her panicked zone. "Have you played before?" he asked her.

Her expression softened, the light returning to her beautiful blue eyes. "When I was younger, my sister and I loved Super Mario," she said softly. "I guess it's a skill you don't forget."

"You certainly didn't." It was as close of a compliment as he could bring himself to give her.

She glanced at him. "Are you hungry? Did you want dinner?"

"My housekeeper left something in the fridge," he said. She was aware he usually ate alone.

"Then am I excused for the day?"

Suddenly he didn't want her to leave, his curiosity about her and the need to learn more and remain in her company riding him hard.

"Join me," he said, the words bursting out unexpectedly.

"I realize I'm paid a salary, but ... dinner. Is it business?" she asked, meeting his gaze. "Because honestly, I'm confused."

He hesitated to admit the truth, but he recognized she was too smart to fall for a lie. He didn't know what to do with the new and confounding feelings he had for her that went beyond sexual. He'd only known her a day, but she'd tapped into the part of him he'd buried after Angela blind-sided him with her deceit. And personal assistant or not, he wasn't ready to let Lexie go.

"I'm not asking you to stay for business. I'm interested in getting to know you better." It was the shocking truth, and for now, he wasn't about to analyze why.

Chapter Three

L EXIE DIDN'T THINK she'd ever been so stunned. On her first day of work, she'd not only held her own with her supposedly tyrannical boss but he'd now expressed interest in her.

Interest she reciprocated. Her mind whirled with conflicting emotions and realities, so she forced herself to recount the truths in her situation.

Fact: It would be stupid to mix business with pleasure.

Fact: Regardless of what was smart, this man intrigued her on a deep level that made her want to know more about him. Like why did he keep himself so withdrawn and apart from the people around him? Why was he so gruff and taciturn? And what did this part of his personality have to do with the photo of him and his brother?

Because no way had he reacted with such anger

just because she'd been looking at an old picture. And she was certain she hadn't imagined the brief hint of longing on his face when he'd stared at the picture. There was much more to Kaden Barnes than the man he showed to the outside world.

Final fact: Bad idea or not, she was already invested, which meant one thing.

She was staying.

She met his gaze and didn't back down from the oh-so-intense look in his vivid green eyes. "So what's for dinner?"

The moment she agreed, the wariness in his expression softened a little. "Let's go find out what Helen left us."

A little while later, he was heating up spaghetti and meatballs on the stove. "My favorite meal," he muttered, as if not wanting to admit to such a tiny personal detail.

"My sister and I used to make spaghetti for dinner. When my mother was too sick to make it downstairs and cook." She retrieved the plates he'd taken out of the cabinet and brought them over to the stove so he could serve the food.

"What was wrong with her?" he asked, deftly placing the pasta on their plates.

"Depression," she said, having long since come to terms with the word.

Some people considered mental illness a stigma, something to be ashamed of. She thought of it as chronic illness, a burden to bear when it wasn't controlled, and merely another facet of someone's life when it was. For her sister, Lexie still had hope.

She didn't, however, know how Kade viewed things. Not wanting to see judgment in his gaze, she busied herself carrying the plates back to the table.

"I'm sorry. It's not easy growing up with any kind of issues dragging you down."

Something about the way he spoke told her not only didn't he judge, he might actually understand.

She raised a shoulder. "It wasn't. It isn't. But when someone is ill, you learn to put them first, no matter what else is going on in life," she said, knowing she was talking about more than her mother. But he didn't need to hear about her sister too.

She picked up the fork and began twirling the long strands.

"I admire that," he said, taking her by surprise.

She swallowed hard, caught up with emotion. "Thank you."

"Not many women—I mean people—would be so selfless."

She glanced away. "Well, I'm not an angel." She lifted the pasta toward her mouth, realizing there were still long pieces attached to the ones on her plate.

She lowered the utensil, shook her head, and began to laugh, breaking the tension between them.

"What's so funny?" he asked.

"Spaghetti is, hands down, the worst date food on the planet. Not that we're on a date," she rushed to correct herself. He was her boss, and though he'd said he wanted to get to know her better, he hadn't elaborated.

And she shouldn't presume. "I mean…"

"I know what you mean." He grinned.

A full-on smile that could only mean he'd dropped his defenses, and it transformed his face. He was sexy at any time, but in this moment, he resembled the young boy in the photo, and she was fully engaged by him.

"Thank you for sharing about your mother," he said, taking her off guard by returning to their previous conversation.

She nodded. "It's not easy to talk about things that hurt you." She deliberately avoided pushing him to open up but hoped he understood she'd listen if he chose to.

"No. But you seem like you'd be a good listener too."

"I am," she said and let it go at that.

Silence ticked by, and he stared into her eyes, the emotional tension slowly turning into something different. The kind of undeniable awareness between a man and a woman who were attracted to one another. And she *was* attracted to this enigmatic man and all his different facets. Especially when he looked at her like he wanted to eat *her* for dinner. Or dessert.

Feeling breathless, even a little aroused, she did what she could to diffuse the desire arcing between them.

"So how about we dig into this meal and stop worrying about who gets sauce on their face?" she said, giving him an easygoing smile.

"Sounds like a plan," he said, that sexy gaze never leaving hers. And as a result, she spent the rest of the evening in a heightened state of sexual desire for a man she had to face in the morning.

As her difficult, demanding boss.

LEXIE ARRIVED AT work the next morning after a night spent tossing and turning, thanks to the afternoon and evening spent with her boss. But he hadn't felt like her boss when she'd confided in him about her mother. Lexie didn't normally talk to people about her problems or her past. Heck, she didn't have any friends left to confide in. No one had patience for the way Lexie chose to live her life.

As she'd insinuated to Kade, she put her sister

first. And that cost her friends she'd stood up or walked out on early when Kendall had needed her. It'd cost her her high school sweetheart, who'd gone to the same college and had stuck around through all of the trials and tribulations that came with Lexie. Until she'd decided to take a leave in order to be there for Kendall during her first hospitalization.

As much as John cared and even tried to understand, he'd wanted her to put her own life first. To put them first. And she just couldn't leave her twin in an institution in another state and focus on school or her own love life. Even the patient John had had his limits. As had any man who'd come after him. Until she no longer bothered to date, putting her love life on hold.

She shook off those thoughts and focused on work, walking in earlier than nine a.m., when Kade was supposed to be in. She stopped by the windows overlooking the city, where the coffeemaker was located, a high-end office Keurig single-serving machine, and carefully mixed three sugars into the black coffee, setting it on her boss's desk at 9:00.

By 9:05, he hadn't arrived, and she dumped the cup, keeping in mind he liked his coffee *hot*. She'd have reheated it in the microwave, but Kade also liked his coffee *fresh*. And nobody else in the office wanted it quite so sweet. She'd asked.

From that point on, she settled in to wait for him

to arrive, keeping an eye on the elevator that opened up directly onto the floor. Her plan was to make the coffee whenever he showed up, and she jumped every time the noise sounded to announce the elevator's arrival. Ten minutes passed. Then twenty.

While she waited, both Lucas's and Derek's personal assistants stopped by her desk to introduce themselves. Everyone was on a first-name basis, including the men in charge, which made for a lighter atmosphere. Their PAs, Tessa and Becky, were both around Lexie's age and extremely friendly. Although they offered their condolences because she was Kade's newest assistant.

She didn't mention that so far she'd held her own with him, aware that his moods could change in an instant as could her standing. She was also afraid any real conversation about her boss would lead to her remembering last night's more personal discussion and the feelings he aroused inside her. She couldn't explain away the blush that was sure to follow.

She glanced at the time on her computer, noting he was half an hour late. He was her boss and had every right to make his own schedule, but because he'd made such a point of mentioning his coffee, her nerves were on edge. And since it was only her second day, and she'd already arranged his work space, she'd need further instruction on what he needed her to do.

So she sat at her desk, one eye—and ear—on the elevator, and twiddled her thumbs.

At nine forty-five, he finally arrived. She made a beeline for the Keurig and prepared his coffee the way he liked it, meeting him at his desk as he unloaded his laptop from the carry case.

She placed the cup down and studied him. He wore a pair of comfortable-looking jeans and a faded beige top with unreadable brown writing. But for the scruff covering his face, he looked more like the incredibly handsome software geek she'd seen last night.

"Morning," he said, finally looking up, a relaxed expression on his face. Obviously he still held a good feeling from their time together yesterday.

So did she.

"Good morning," she said, standing in front of the aluminum desk.

He lowered himself into his plush leather seat, immediately picking up his coffee and taking a sip. "Hot and fresh. You're already ahead of my last assistant," he said, sounding surprised.

"What time is it?" she asked him.

He glanced at his Apple watch. "Nine forty-six," he replied. "Why?"

"Well, I have a suggestion ... assuming you're open to one."

He cocked an eyebrow, folding his arms across his chest. "Go on."

She swallowed hard. On hiring her, Derek had specifically told her not to let him intimidate her and to do what she thought was best for him. She pulled that information around her now.

"I realize you're the boss and can make your own hours, but you told me you'd be in at nine. You also said you like your coffee fresh and hot—"

"Which I just complimented you on, so what's wrong?"

"It's just that it would be more convenient for your assistant—me—to know what time you plan on coming in. Considering you like to have your coffee on your desk, *fresh and hot* when you arrive. I jumped up every time the elevator dinged. I was beginning to feel like a Mexican jumping bean."

"Your point?"

She smoothed her hand over the shiny desktop before meeting his gaze. "If you're going to be late, I'd appreciate a call or a text. This way I know and can arrange your schedule—and your coffee—accordingly."

He reached into his front jeans pocket and curled his hand around whatever object he'd retrieved. "Here," he muttered, depositing a key down on the desk. "I change the lock to my apartment after each assistant leaves."

"Must be a full-time job," she quipped, realizing too late she shouldn't have let that joke slip.

To her surprise, his lips twitched in a near smile, and that tiny gesture gave her immense pleasure.

"I stopped at a locksmith on the way here so I could make you a copy," he said. "To facilitate your job. Not to make it more difficult."

"Thank you," she said softly.

He met her gaze, those green eyes warmer than she was used to. "You're welcome."

She sighed, her suddenly needy body swaying closer even though he was a full desk away. She jerked herself upright, forcibly shaking herself out of the spell he effortlessly wove around her.

She cleared her throat. "After you're settled in, I'd like to go over my duties and how you handle your appointments and calendar. Things like that." She cursed the huskiness in her voice caused from just a near smile. Man, either she was sex-starved or in big trouble.

"Give me a few minutes and I'll call you in," he said gruffly.

She inclined her head, turned, and started for the door.

"Lexie," he said, the rough timbre of his voice sending more shivers of awareness rushing through her.

She grasped the doorframe, and yes, she squeezed her thighs together, because her body reacted to his use of her name, her panties growing damp.

"Yes?" She glanced over her shoulder, meeting his gaze.

"Point taken. Next time I'm going to be late, I'll let you know." No sooner had he spoken than he looked down, busying himself on his cell.

Stunned, she walked back to her desk on trembling legs … and waited for him to call her in to work.

A few minutes later, Derek and Lucas walked into his office and slammed the door behind them, giving her more time to wait. And to think about Kade, the man who seemed to be softening … and she hadn't even been here long.

KADE WAS DRINKING the best damned cup of coffee he'd ever had just because Lexie had it made as soon as he'd walked in the door. He leaned back against his chair, feet on his desk. He was unfamiliar with the emotions coursing through him. From pleasure at seeing her in his office to appreciating how she'd picked up on his needs.

Yeah, he'd told his other assistants that he wanted his coffee hot and fresh as soon as he arrived in the morning, but somehow they'd all screwed it up. And though it was just coffee, he understood the need was as much a part of his routine as the way he put on his socks, right foot, then left, or brushed his teeth, also right side, then left.

But Lexie seemed to roll with his demands despite the fact that he could be a pain in the ass. The truth was, there was also part of him that liked to see how far he could push people before they walked away ... because they always did.

Except for Derek, Luke, and once upon a time, Julian. Brothers in fraternity and in reality. Julian had chosen drugs over his best friends. Demons and addiction had driven him. Kade didn't worry about anything pulling Derek and Luke away. They were solid. They were his family.

Now there was this spitfire of a woman who'd barreled into his life twenty-four hours ago, and he couldn't think of anything else. He'd be a damned liar if he didn't admit that after she'd left, her scent lingering in his apartment, he'd wrapped his fingers around his cock and brought himself much-needed relief. He'd come all over his hand like a horny adolescent, Lexie's face in his mind, imagining it was her body he was fucking instead of his hand.

He tried to remind himself that she worked for him, but he couldn't bring himself to care. He still wanted her. Just as he knew she could and probably would let him down.

Without warning, his office door banged open, hitting the wall behind it, and his partners stormed in.

Derek took one look at him and asked, "What's with that grin on your face?"

Feeling like an ass, Kade ignored the comment. "What's wrong?" Because they hadn't come barreling in for no reason.

"We have a fucking problem," Luke said.

Derek slammed the door shut and hit the lock. That meant shit just got real. "What's going on?"

The two men glanced at each other.

"Just spit it out," Kade ordered them, not enjoying being in the dark.

"Somehow Julian *knows*," Derek said. "And this company and everything we've worked for is in jeopardy." He didn't need to elaborate.

There was only one thing Julian could have uncovered that would threaten everything they'd built—were building.

Kade was the weak link and he knew it. "How?" he asked his friends.

"He hired a PI who went digging through your past."

Kade didn't have to ask why Julian had gone after him and not the others. When shit had gone down with Julian, it was Kade who'd stood by him the longest ... until he hadn't. Couldn't. Not anymore. Once he'd sided with Derek and Luke, agreeing that Julian's refusal to get treatment would only drag their business down, Julian had been thrown out of anything to do with Blink—and the money that came with it.

Julian made it clear he blamed Kade. Because he'd been closer to Kade than to the other two men. It was Kade on whom he'd seek revenge.

Although Kade's father had tried to make certain the past stayed buried, nothing was foolproof.

"How did he uncover the information?" Kade asked.

Derek ran a hand through his dark hair. "He found Lila."

"Fuck!" Kade slammed his hand into the wall, not caring about the consequences.

"Hey, man, calm down. We'll counter anything he throws at us," Luke said, coming up behind him and putting a hand on his shoulder.

"Really? We're taking this company public. You think a date rape accusation against one of the CEOs won't hurt? No matter how false it is?" His breath caught in his throat, panic surfacing along with the memories.

He'd been twenty-one and a cocky college junior,

home from school for Thanksgiving break, and determined to break free from the geek stigma he'd been nailed with in high school, like he already had in college. He'd met Lila at a neighborhood bar. He'd been attracted to her the minute she walked through the door, with her short skirt and *I'm available* attitude.

They'd fucked that night and he'd felt like a king. Until her parents showed up at Kade's house, accusing him of raping their daughter. When she'd come home the night before, her controlling father was waiting up, figured out she'd been with a guy, and turned furious. She'd claimed Kade had drugged and raped her.

Kade had wanted to fight the bullshit accusation, but his father preferred to pay in order to make problems go away. Without Kade's knowledge, he'd gone to Lila's parents and thrown money at them to prevent his son from being arrested and put in jail, the rest of his life ruined.

Except Kade knew he hadn't drugged or raped the girl, and going to the cops would have at least proved she'd lied about being slipped a roofie. There was no evidence now beyond *he said, she said*. He'd begged his father not to pay them off. But Keith Barnes had spent his life trying to make it up to Kade for losing his mother and brother. He thought money fixed all things, and there'd been no deterring him. He'd paid off the family.

Kade's father wasn't an idiot. He'd had the parents sign a nondisclosure agreement. But they could have run through the money, or Julian, the bastard, could have offered them even more to snitch.

Fast forward to today—*he said, she said* was enough to scare off potential shareholders in his soon-to-be public company. So was the payoff. Everyone would assume Kade had something to hide. For all these reasons, he'd confided in Derek and Luke just last year. He felt they needed to know before they took this company to the next level. They'd immediately stood by him.

"Breathe, man," Luke said. "We're going to get enough on Julian to bury him. That'll ensure this stays dead and buried too. I already called Evan Mann. He's a PI with a solid rep. We'll get this sorted," he assured him.

Kade breathed out hard, trying not to panic. The notion of a rape charge wasn't something he wanted to revisit ... and there was a twenty-five-year statute of limitations on sex crimes. He wasn't close to out of the woods if Lila and her parents decided to make things ugly and press charges. They'd be as money hungry as Julian, out to get a piece of Kade ... and Blink.

Suddenly his hand began to throb, and he cursed out loud, looking down at his swollen, bruised knuckles.

"Shit. That could be broken," Derek said, having joined them on Kade's side of the desk.

"You should have it x-rayed," Luke said in agreement.

Normally Kade would balk at going to the doctor, but the way this mother hurt… "Yeah, okay."

"I'd join you but I have a meeting with a new developer," Luke said. "Derek is sitting in."

"Then it's a good thing Kade has a personal assistant he likes so much. She can go along for the ride," Derek said with a shit-eating grin on his face.

Luke shook his head and walked across the room, unlocking and opening the door. "Lexie get in here!" he called before Kade, with his excruciating pain, could process what he was doing.

Lexie rushed into the room. "Is everything okay?" she asked, her voice filled with concern. Her gaze immediately rested on Kade, who cradled his injured hand with the other. "Oh my God! What did you do?"

"He had an accident," Derek said. "Can you get us some ice? And call for a car. You're going to need to accompany him to the emergency room for X-rays."

"Of course." She spared a worried glance at Kade before rushing out.

"Thanks for that," Kade muttered. Now Lexie had proof he wasn't just a pain in the ass, he had a temper as well. Except he didn't. Fear had driven him to this jacked move.

"We'll handle things here. Get the hand looked at and go home. Let your new assistant take care of you," Derek instructed, that same pleased grin on his face.

"If I didn't know better, I'd think you were playing matchmaker," Kade muttered.

"Who said I'm not?" Derek asked, just as Lexie returned with a bag full of ice, her timing impeccable.

Her presence very needed. As much as the reminder of the past had Kade wanting to close out the world and shut down, he couldn't deny he'd much rather turn to Lexie for comfort. And much more.

Chapter Four

L EXIE RUSHED DOWNSTAIRS and retrieved ice in a bag from a restaurant nearby, then headed back to Kade's office in record time. Derek and Luke must have left, so she walked up to Kade, who stood staring out the window, as if he hadn't heard her come in.

"Can I see your hand?" she asked softly.

He turned around, and the raw pain in his face stole her breath. Without speaking, he held out his hand. His knuckles were swollen and bruised, already a deep purple. She lightly rested the bottom of his palm in hers and gently put the ice over the top.

"I'll call for a car, and we can head over to the hospital," she said without pushing for answers as to why he'd gotten so angry the plaster on the wall behind him was cracked. She hoped he'd confide in her eventually because he seemed like he had a lot to get off his chest.

"You don't have to go along. I'm capable of taking myself."

"I'm sure you are." She sensed this man was an island. He thought he liked it that way. He just didn't know any other way.

"But I want to help." She glanced down at his ice-covered hand, rotating the bag so as not to overdo any one spot. "Put your free hand here and I'll arrange for a car."

She'd found a helpful list of various things, left behind by one of the former assistants. Car service had been on it.

He placed his hand over the ice, brushing her skin as they switched positions. Electricity—inappropriate and so wrongly timed—rushed over her, causing the hair on her arms to stand on end.

They made the trip to the closest hospital in silence, Kade's clenched jaw an indication of his pain. And because this was a typical emergency room and since a bruised hand wasn't triaged as urgent, they waited for hours, surrounded by sick people who used the ER as a doctor's office.

Hacking coughs, lots of noses being blown loudly, a knife-wound victim with blood trailing behind the injured man, and the topper, the child vomiting in the corner.

Squicked out, Lexie inched closer to Kade, afraid

of catching anything. But she was determined to stick it out and get him that X-ray. She wasn't a doctor, but those knuckles looked *bad*. She held her tongue and tempered her frustration at how long they had to wait.

Not Kade. He complained. Bitched. And finally tried to bully and ultimately bribe the triage nurse to let him pass before she threatened to call security and have him thrown out on his ass.

Lexie got in his face with a wagging finger. "Look, you might be used to preferential treatment most of the time, but here you're less important than someone having a heart attack. Deal with it," she ordered, feeling every inch the shrew as she lectured him. He deserved it.

"You're bossy," he muttered.

"But I get the job done." She folded her arms across her chest and, with a glare, dared him to comment.

He didn't. Instead he focused on the fresh ice the nurse had given him.

His compliance lasted another hour before he rose to leave. "That's it. I'm done. The pain's not that bad anymore."

"Liar." She scowled at him, then physically grabbed his arm on the uninjured side and pulled him back to his seat. "Quit making a scene, and I'll go ask if they have any idea how much longer it might be."

Before she could do as she promised, a male nurse stepped through the double doors. "Barnes? Kaden Barnes."

"Thank God," Lexie muttered, remaining seated when Kade stood.

"This way," the nurse gestured.

Kade glanced at her. "Well? Let's go."

She shook her head. "They're not going to let me go into X-ray with you. I'll be here when you get out."

"They're just going to take me into a room and make me wait some more. You're coming."

She shrugged and rose to follow, surprised and secretly delighted that he wanted her with him. The nurse didn't argue, so she soon found herself in a curtained cubicle as Kade had predicted. After the expected wait, a doctor finally came in to examine him.

Lexie winced along with Kade as the doctor lifted the hand and attempted to move fingers and thoroughly looked at the injury. "I'm pretty certain it's a Boxer's Fracture, a result of a break in the metacarpal when the bones hit a hard, immovable object." He glanced at Kade as if waiting for an explanation as to how he'd gotten the injury.

When none came, the man shrugged and called a nurse to take him to X-ray. He allowed Lexie to wait in the cubicle.

While he was gone, Lexie called her sister to check

in. The call went straight to voice mail, and she left a message, requesting Kendall call her back.

Kade finally returned, which led to another long wait for a doctor to come in with the results.

"Thank you," Kade said into the prolonged silence.

"You're welcome." She almost told him she was just doing her job but stopped herself because that would have been a lie. True, Derek and Luke had asked her to go along, but she would have anyway and not because she was Kade's personal assistant.

Because in a very short time, she was coming to care about him, and that was something she couldn't let happen. She already had firsthand experience of what happened when she didn't put a man first in her life. And a demanding man like Kade? He'd have no patience for her sister or her issues, no matter how kind he'd been when she'd told him the truth about her mother.

With a little luck, Kendall's meds would kick in, and this would be the time things stuck. She'd turn herself around and get her life back on track. Then Lexie could focus on herself. Even if Kade was truly interested in her now, the sad truth was that said interest would fade long before that ever happened. The thought caused a pain in the pit of her stomach.

"Mr. Barnes." The doctor pushed his way through

the curtain. "I have your X-ray results, and it's just as I expected, a Boxer's Fracture. I'm going to splint the hand and fingers. I think we can avoid casting the entire arm up to the elbow."

"Thank God." Kade let out a groan of relief.

"That said, you need to keep the hand and arm immobilized as much as possible so it heals. Follow up with an orthopedist within the week. No lifting or stress on the hand or you risk injuring surrounding blood vessels, tendons, ligaments, and nerves. And keep the splint dry."

The splint covered his entire hand, keeping his pinky and ring finger in place. The bruising on the knuckles of the other two fingers was still visible.

He was going to be in pain, something the doctor confirmed when he wrote up a prescription for painkillers. "If those make you sick, ibuprofen or acetaminophen might take the edge off. But for the first twenty-four hours, try to take the prescription as written and use the ice."

"Thank you," Kade said, sounding deflated at all the restrictions and issues he'd caused himself.

When the doctor finally left, Kade turned to Lexie. "Can you let Derek and Luke know the results?"

She nodded. "Of course. Is your housekeeper there to help you with meals?" Lexie asked.

"I'll be fine."

She frowned, not liking the idea of him going home alone, taking painkillers, and doing too much with his dominant, injured hand. "I'll come back with you and help you get settled," she decided out loud, reassuring herself it was the right thing to do.

"On the clock?" he asked.

Surprised by the question, her gaze shot to his only to find him grinning at her, and she realized he was mimicking her similar question of the night before. He'd asked her to stay for dinner, and she'd wanted to know if it was business. He wanted to know the same thing now.

"No," she admitted, not questioning herself too much. Because she knew she wouldn't like the direction the truth would take her.

With her sister's issues, Lexie didn't have time for a real relationship. She couldn't afford messy feelings for her boss. And though she feared that was exactly where she was headed, she knew nothing could come of it as long as she had to put Kendall first.

It was, Lexie thought, the story of her life.

KADE SETTLED IN on his couch, reclining the chair and trying to get comfortable despite the raging pain in his hand. Although he hadn't wanted to take the narcotic the doctor had prescribed and deal with feeling woozy, Lexie had insisted. And with the pain increasing, especially after how the X-ray tech had manipulated his hand, Kade had finally agreed.

Lexie had the driver stop for a hamburger from McDonald's so he didn't take the pill on an empty stomach and then watched as he swallowed. She was the ultimate caregiver, something he'd never experienced in any woman before.

Though she was his PA, any way he sliced it, this wasn't in her job description. Then again, he was light-headed and feeling no pain due to the narcotic. His judgment probably couldn't be trusted at the moment. He kind of liked the feeling of not worrying about a damned thing.

He picked up the remote and flipped through the channels, settling on a movie he couldn't name. His head spun, and he saw two of everything on the screen. Nice, he thought, leaning back against the headrest.

"Here are some things I thought you might need," Lexie said, walking in from the kitchen, carrying a bottle of water and a bag of Twizzlers. "Your favorite." She smiled and placed the items on the tray between two seats. "Can I open the bag for you?"

He nodded, realizing for the first time how immobile and ineffectual he would be. "This was really an asshole move," he muttered. "I can't believe this." He gestured to the hand he was icing with his good one.

She curled into the chair next to him, tucking her legs primly beneath her. She opened the bag and handed him a piece of the red candy. He took a bite, savoring the burst of cherry flavor.

"So … anything you want to get off your chest?" she asked. "Like *why* you felt the need to punch the wall?"

His mind wandered, from his past to Julian. "Assholes. I'm frustrated by assholes."

She waited patiently, which was a good thing, because his brain was like mush, and he had to search for his thoughts. "An old friend is suing us for a stake in the company and for the money we'll get upon taking Blink public."

"I read about the lawsuit," she admitted. "Does he have a case?"

"Fucking lawyers said he's got enough to stand on that we should settle. And now Julian's dug up old dirt on me. He found a girl who claims I raped her in college." The words came out fuzzy to his ears.

"What? No!" Lexie said, immediately coming to his defense, which, addled brain or not, managed to surprise him. Her blue eyes widened in horror, but he instinctively knew it wasn't at him.

"How do you know?" he asked.

She grabbed his good hand, leaning over the divider between the two seats, and met his gaze. "I just do. I trust my instincts. Always have. And you might be an arrogant ass and an occasional jerk, but you're not a rapist!"

"Tell it to the judge," he muttered.

She still held his hand as she moved in closer. "I would if I could."

And he'd let her.

Because nobody had automatically believed him before. Nobody stood up for him without question. His father's words, when he'd found out about the date rape accusation, were, *It doesn't matter, son. I'll take care of you.*

Which was all well and good, except it had mattered to Kade. He'd been innocent and wanted to prove it, not throw money at the situation to make it go away. Ironically, all he'd done was make Kade feel more alone.

Not Lexie. She made him feel good about himself for the first time in a long time. He wanted more. Without hesitation, he closed the distance between them and pressed his mouth against hers. She startled, jerking in surprise, before almost immediately giving in, her lips softening against his. He breathed her in, both her warm breath and her intoxicating belief in him.

He ran his tongue over her lips. Though he was

confined by the wide armrests between them and his own injury, he was every bit engaged. Just ask his body. Painkillers had no effect on his cock, because it was hard and ready to go.

He wanted to lift his hand and cup the back of her neck, pull her closer, kiss her harder, but he was hindered by the need to keep his bad hand away from the furniture and any pressure against it. Instead he made good use of his tongue, delving deep into her mouth and tasting her sweetness.

"Mmm," he murmured against her mouth because she was incredibly sweet, her flavor making him even more light-headed than before.

"Kade." She placed a gentle hand on his shoulder. "We shouldn't."

"Can't think of a reason why not." Other than the dizziness circling his brain, but she didn't know about that.

"I work for you, for one thing. And you're hurting. Your defenses are down. Something tells me you might agree with me come morning and regret this."

"Never." It was the last thought he had before he passed out cold, dreaming of a blue-eyed, brown-haired angel who came to his rescue.

KADE WOKE UP with a blistering headache and

throbbing in his hand. He waited for the awareness of the pain to settle before he rolled to a sitting position. He hung his spinning head, bracing his good hand on his thigh.

How had he gotten into bed? The last thing he remembered was chewing on a Twizzler, then ... confiding in and kissing Lexie.

"Fuck!"

"You're up." Derek strode into his bedroom, his hair a mess, wearing a pair of track pants and a tee shirt, looking like he'd spent the night.

"What are you doing here?" Kade asked.

"Aww. You don't remember me tucking you into bed last night? I'm hurt." Derek smirked at his own joke.

"No, I don't."

He sat down on the end of the mattress. "Lexie called. Asked me to come help move your passed-out ass into bed. She had to get home, so I stayed in case you needed something."

Kade shot him a grateful look. "Thanks, man."

"Not a problem. Are you hurting?"

"Badly, but I'm not taking anything stronger than ibuprofen."

Derek narrowed his gaze. "Why suffer if you don't have to?"

Kade didn't often spill his guts with a clear head,

but when he did it was to this man. "Because apparently I talk too much when I'm drugged."

"Ouch." Derek winced.

Yeah. The memory came back to him with too much clarity considering the fuzziness he'd been experiencing while opening his big mouth. He'd told Lexie that he'd been accused of date rape. Exposed not just himself but his partners to another person who could use the information against them. God. He'd have to handle her ASAP, make sure she understood the gravity of the information she held.

Recalling his gut-spilling made him antsy, and he reached for the Patek Philipe watch, the first piece he'd bought with his own hard-earned money from Blink. Holding it steady against his hurt hand, he pulled out the crown and began to wind the watch. It was a difficult endeavor with his hand, but he'd learned early on that the motion soothed him. He had other watches that he wore more often now, but he kept this one on his nightstand and wound it daily when he woke up.

"Pop the crown back in?" he asked Derek, who took the watch and did as Kade asked before handing it back.

Kade placed the timepiece on his nightstand and ran his good hand over his dry eyes, feeling marginally better about what he'd told Lexie. He didn't want to think she'd betray him, but he'd been wrong about women before. Still, he didn't want to give Derek any more to worry about, so he didn't go into detail.

"Was talking all you two did?" Derek asked. "Because when I showed up, Lexie was flustered, and she looked like a woman who'd been well kissed." He grinned. "I have to give you credit. Even doped up, you managed to make a move. You're slick, I'll give you that."

Kade rolled his eyes, refusing to give his friend the satisfaction of a reply. The fact was, Kade hadn't been slick, he'd been, as Derek said, drugged. With his defenses down due to the narcotic, he'd kissed Lexie and enjoyed every damned second.

He had a thing for sweets and could get addicted to her honeyed taste very quickly—if he let himself. But this morning his barriers and his brain were functioning again, and he couldn't let any woman get inside his head.

No matter how much he liked Lexie, he couldn't allow himself to forget hard-won lessons. Women screwed him over.

"She's not like her," Derek said, interrupting his thoughts.

"Who's not like who?" Kade asked. Because he had so many women who'd betrayed him in his background, he actually had his pick.

His mother, the woman who was supposed to take care of him but had walked out on him instead. Lila with her date rape accusation. And Angela, his girlfriend just as Blink was gaining popularity, who'd enjoyed the money his father sent him and the things Kade bought her but was selling them for cash instead … stealing from him at the same time she was pretending to be in love.

Derek rose to a standing position. "I was going to say Lexie's not like Lila, but since you obviously have them all on the brain, she's not like any of the females in your past. She's a woman who needs a job, is capable of putting up with your shit, and knows how to handle you."

"Maybe." He ran a hand over his short hair. He'd like to think Derek was right about Lexie. "But I can't take the risk."

Derek groaned. "You are a fucking hard nut to crack. Okay, fine. Have it your way. Are you coming to work today?"

"Yeah." Even if he got nothing accomplished, he'd rather keep himself busy there than be alone here with too much time to think—about Lexie, why he couldn't take things any further, and what in the hell he was going to do about her now.

I KISSED MY boss and I liked it. The refrain had run through Lexie's head ever since leaving Kade's apartment. Running from it, actually, without looking back. She knew Derek would take care of his friend, and she'd needed to get away, but that kiss had followed her … home and into her dreams.

She fell asleep with the feel of his lips on hers, the cherry taste of his mouth lingering, and she dreamt of much more than a kiss—her entire body was engaged, her hands dragging up his shirt, molding over his hard chest and defined ab muscles. Her breasts were heavy, her nipples hard because he was tweaking them with his hands. Big hands, large enough to cup her heavy breasts, palm them, and make her feel heaven with his touch.

She woke up aching and empty, her panties soaked with evidence of her desire for a man she shouldn't want. Couldn't have. And had to face this morning.

She chose her wardrobe like armor today, picking a pair of loose trousers that didn't define her curves, a man-tailored blouse, and a pair of medium heels. Nothing sexy about it, she thought as she sat at her desk, waiting for the ding of the elevator and a glimpse of Kade's dark hair.

Dark brown hair she dreamed of running her fingers through, though in reality it was too short for that. When her nipples started to tighten, she wrapped her hands around her cold bottle of water, hoping to stop any further hot, inappropriate thoughts.

As if she could.

It was almost a relief when he stepped off the elevator and she could put the awkward first hello behind her. She rose and immediately made his coffee, only to find they were out of the strong brew K-cups. She grabbed the Breakfast Blend, knowing it was a lighter flavor, and hoped for the best, mixing it exactly the way he liked it.

She stepped into the doorway of his office. Holding her breath, she knocked once to catch his attention.

He turned, meeting her gaze with a cool look that didn't bode well for her. Obviously he didn't want to face the intimate moment they'd shared any more than she did. Well, that was okay. Maybe they could pretend it hadn't happened and go on with their day. A girl could dream, she thought.

Stomach fluttering, she walked into the office. The sun streamed through the window, showcasing a breathtaking view of the city. Unfortunately for her, she couldn't stop staring at him. His eyes were bloodshot from lack of a good night's sleep and obvious pain, and despite it all, her heart clenched. She felt for him, knowing he was suffering both physically and emotionally.

"How's your hand?" she asked him.

"Hurts." He paused, and awkward silence surrounded them. Finally, he spoke again. "Thanks for yesterday," he said, gruff words strained, but she appreciated them anyway.

"You're welcome. Can I help you with anything?" She gestured around his desk, knowing he was at a disadvantage with one hand out of commission.

He shook his head. "Just leave the coffee on the desk. I have a call in a few minutes and I need privacy. I'll shoot you an email with a to-do list later."

"Umm…" She glanced at his bandaged, splinted hand. "Unless you want to peck out the keys, why don't you just call me in when you're off the phone. I can take notes on what you'd like me to do."

"I'm not an invalid. Don't treat me like one."

No, he was just a rude ass. "Suit yourself," she muttered.

She turned and headed back to her desk, under no delusions about his behavior. He was being obnoxious on purpose, freezing her out because she'd dared to get close to him yesterday.

She blew out a deep breath. Part of her understood. With her family history, she didn't let people in either. Her mother or sister was always bound to do something disruptive and throw off the balance of Lexie's life. She'd learned most people didn't understand, and it was easier to be a loner than to lose friends.

Still, she had to admit it hurt to have Kade do the same to her. Even if he had his reasons—like regretting that he'd confided in her about his past. Or kissing her. That one hurt more.

She glanced at her cell phone, surprised to see a text message from Kendall. She'd been in the kitchen when Lexie left for work, basically ignoring any questions Lexie asked her. From *Any luck looking for a job?* to the benign *What are you doing today?* she'd been met with silence.

She glanced at her cell screen.

Kendall: *I'm sorry I've been such a bitch to you.*

Lexie was used to the cycle of anger and apology and typed in her reply: *Thank you. Hope you have a good day.* She didn't have the time or the inclination to argue while at work.

Kendall: *Need my meds adjusted. Dr. Kay has a twelve p.m. Come along? Don't want to go alone.*

Lexie leaned back in her chair and groaned, trying her best to ignore the twisting in her stomach caused by being pulled in two directions. Work versus family. She swallowed hard and glanced at her watch. As long as she was given a lunch break, she could meet up with Kendall for her appointment and be back here in time to work.

Counting on a normal workday, she texted her sister back: *Will meet you there. Have to go back to work after.*

Kendall: *Thx. U R the best.*

No, she was a sucker for her needy twin, but what else could she do?

"Lexie!" Kade yelled from inside his office.

She jumped up fast, wondering if he'd done something to hurt his hand. "What's wrong?" she asked, nearly tripping over herself to get there quickly.

"My coffee's cold and weak," he said, a displeased look on his face.

That was all? "You're out of the kind you prefer, so it's a lighter blend. And I made it fifteen minutes ago. If you're just drinking it now, of course it's gone cold. I'll just go make another one," she said, keeping her voice pleasant.

"Make sure we have the right kind tomorrow," he snapped.

She somehow refrained from saluting. "Anything else?" she asked.

"It's not sweet enough."

She ground her teeth before answering. "It has three sugars. Unless you want to go into a diabetic coma, I'm sure it's plenty sweet."

He frowned. "Well, bring me an extra packet, just in case."

She stepped closer to the desk, knowing she was

about to poke the bear. "Do you think maybe something else is bothering you besides the coffee?" she asked in a deliberately *sugary* voice. Pun intended.

He stiffened. "I don't know what you mean."

She walked closer to the desk, placing one hand on the cool aluminum surface, because she didn't want their raised voices causing office gossip.

"Instead of being a jerk about the coffee, how about you face the fact that we kissed last night?" Ignoring her trembling insides, she met his gaze, determined to hold her own. "And maybe you're upset because you told me some things you wish you hadn't?" she pushed on.

"Un-fucking-believable." He stormed around her and walked to the door, slamming it closed so they were well and truly alone.

Chapter Five

KADE TURNED TO face Lexie, not feeling the least bit professional as he reined in his frustration and desire. The damned woman was always one step ahead of him, figuring him out and calling him on his behavior. And today, she'd nailed him. He was being a complete and utter ass because he'd crossed the line with his personal assistant, kissed her, and trusted her with information that shouldn't have left this office.

He couldn't let her know she got to him beyond the superficial. "You really think you have me figured out?" he asked.

"We both know I do. Look, if it makes you feel any better, I'm no more ready to deal with anything between us than you are. My life is too complicated, so we can just forget the kiss ever happened."

Her words cut deep. Even if she had her reasons, she didn't want to deal with him. She wanted to forget, and that was something women in his life were good at.

But a glance at her flushed cheeks told him that he had affected her. For the first time today, he raked his gaze over her from top to bottom. Instead of a sexy skirt, she wore a pair of trousers that hid her shape, a boxy shirt that would have looked better on him, and very little makeup. She was hiding. Which told him she'd been every bit as unnerved by that kiss as he was.

He stepped closer, and she inched back, the dance continuing until she came up against the wall and he sandwiched her there, close enough to be in her personal space and breach her comfort zone. Her heavy breasts rose and fell beneath that god-awful shirt, her nipples poking through the material.

Need sliced through him at the sight. And then she pulled her bottom lip between her teeth, and he ached to do the same, to have the freedom to taste her again, to cup those breasts and feel their weight in his hands.

But he couldn't. And she needed to understand she wasn't the one calling the shots or defining whatever this was between them.

"Lexie, I don't have any desire for a relationship either." She hadn't used the word, but he might as well make himself perfectly clear. "I don't know what's going on in your life, but mine is equally complicated, if not more so. So I'm sorry if a kiss while under the influence of drugs gave you the wrong impression," he said dismissively.

Which was ironic because, as he stepped back, it was with great difficulty, and under duress thanks to his cock, which protested him pushing her away.

She glared at him. "*Under the influence.* You're going to blame one lousy painkiller instead of owning your actions?" she asked, her eyes flashing with hurt and anger.

"I am," he said, even if, deep down, he knew, as she did, that the kiss had been inevitable.

That at some point, given their chemistry, he'd have taken her into his arms … and done more than kiss her if his injured hand hadn't prevented it. But if the painkiller gave him an excuse, so be it.

Now, when she was off-balance, he had to go in for the kill. "As for the information I admitted to, also while under the influence…" He didn't use the words *date rape*. He couldn't.

She narrowed her gaze. "What about it?"

"I'd like you to sign this." He strode over to his desk and pulled up the paper he'd printed as soon as he'd arrived this morning, having come up with the solution on the way to work.

"What is it?" she asked warily.

"A nondisclosure agreement." He handed her the

one-page document. "It guarantees you won't speak of or repeat what you learn in the context of our … business relationship. That includes whatever you learn here or while in my apartment."

She sucked in a startled breath, a slight gasp coming out too. "You don't trust me not to repeat what you told me last night. After I brought you home, fed you, took care of you, and made sure you weren't alone and in pain, you're going to repay me by asking me to sign an NDA," she said, her voice cracking as she spoke.

His hand began to throb, and he realized he'd been letting it hang down, the blood flowing into his injured knuckles and fingers. Damned if he didn't deserve it.

"It's standard procedure in business," he said.

"Then you should have included it in the packet Derek gave me when I signed on after he hired me." She stormed over to the desk, pulled out a pen, and scrawled her name on the page. "Here." She turned and slapped the paper against his chest.

Damned if he didn't admire her spunk and the way she stood up to him, acting as if they were still in his apartment last night and not here at work. True, he was her boss, but he'd mixed business and pleasure, and she'd more than earned the right to speak her mind. Just this once, he told himself, he'd let her get away with talking to him this way.

"Thank you." He placed the paper on his desk.

She started for the door, then turned back to face him. "You know, if you'd come to me and asked me nicely to sign, I wouldn't have had a problem. If you'd accepted the fact that we both wanted that kiss but it couldn't happen again, I wouldn't be angry. Instead you came up with a bunch of excuses, insulted me personally, and questioned my integrity. Very nice, Mr. Barnes."

His stomach churned with every word she spoke, and he hated himself for how he'd handled things. Just because he couldn't deal with getting close to a woman didn't mean she had to pay the price.

At his unexpected line of thinking, he furrowed his brow. Since when did he think twice about doing what needed to be done in business or in his personal life? Why was he so bothered by the hurt in her eyes, the pained expression on her face? She was just an employee, he reminded himself, and he'd fired and yelled at plenty before her. He just didn't like doing it to Lexie. Which was all the more reason for him to cut things off now, before he allowed his guard down further, began to believe in her, trust her ... and ended up gutted again.

"You know what else?" she asked.

He knew exactly what was coming next. He'd been in this position before. "You're quitting," he said before she could.

His stomach twisted, and the coffee he'd been drinking threatened to come back up. Fuck. Too late, he realized her departure wasn't what he wanted. Hell, when it came to Lexie, he didn't know what he wanted.

She let out a harsh laugh. "No, I'm not quitting. You don't get to be that lucky. I said I could handle you and I will. My error was thinking there was a caring human being behind the jerk façade. I won't make that mistake again. Unless…"

She trailed off, her eyes widening. "Are you firing me?" she asked, suddenly sounding worried, and he remembered Derek mentioning she needed the job.

He just hadn't asked him why. God, Kade thought, he really was a jerk.

"Are you?" she asked, voice rising when he didn't answer immediately.

He couldn't. He'd been too busy processing the fact that he hadn't driven her away.

"No," he finally said. "I'm not firing you." He didn't want her gone.

But he damned well better figure out what exactly he did want from Lexie Parker before they drove each other insane.

LEXIE'S HEART BEAT hard in her chest as she settled in to work. She was used to confrontation with her sister. Not so much with other people, but she couldn't let Kade treat her so badly, not for any reason. It hurt her feelings that he thought he could.

A to-do list showed up in her email, and Lexie spent the next hour handling appointments and other research information points for Kade. If that's how he wanted to communicate, then fine. When lunchtime arrived, she emailed him she was going out and would be back in an hour.

On her way to the elevator, she heard her name being called.

She turned to find Tessa, a perky blonde, and Becky, a redhead with pretty green eyes, catching up with her. "We're going out for lunch too. Want to join us?" Becky, Derek's assistant, asked.

Lexie really did, but of course, she had to be at her sister's doctor's appointment. "I wish I could but I have an appointment I can't cancel. Rain check?" she asked hopefully.

Tessa nodded. "Of course. Oh! We're going out Friday night. There's a bar called Lights around the corner. Want to come along?"

She mentally scanned her calendar, and as far as she knew, she was free on Friday. "I'd love to."

"Yay! Dress funky," Becky said as the elevator

opened. "We'll get toasted and have fun."

"I'm looking forward to it." She really was.

These women were doing their best to make Lexie feel welcome, and she appreciated the effort more than she could express. It had been a long time since she'd had a group of girlfriends of any kind, and she promised herself she'd do everything in her power to show up, be present, and not have to leave early for a Kendall rescue.

To Lexie's relief, Kendall's appointment went smoothly. Her sister really seemed to want to feel better and had taken the initiative by scheduling a meeting with her doctor. For the first time in a long time, Lexie had hope that her sister would improve.

She wasn't sure what hope she had for any kind of relationship with her boss. For the rest of the week, they communicated by text or email, and he grunted thank you for his morning coffee. She picked up his dry cleaning and dropped it off at his apartment after work, to find he wasn't at home. She made sure his lunch was prepared the way he liked it and sat in on meetings with potential investors for the app. But there was no real communication between them, their relationship barely professional.

By Friday, there was no thaw or change. It bothered her on all levels because she didn't like living or working in an armed-camp-like state. What frustrated her most of all, however, was that her anger at him didn't dull the desire she experienced every time she looked at him. It wasn't just that he oozed sex appeal, but she remembered their kiss vividly and knew what kind of chemistry they shared. None of that mattered, however, because he was her boss. Even if they were getting along great, she couldn't cross that line again.

She was glad Becky and Tessa had invited her out tonight. She needed a break from routine. It would be good for her to go out, have a drink or two, and just have fun for once in her structured life. And if she was really lucky, she wouldn't think about Kaden Barnes at all.

KADE LET LUKE and Derek drag him out to his favorite steak house for dinner. They hit this place at least once a month, and Kade always picked up from here on Helen's day off, when he was responsible for his own supper. He'd planned on hanging out in front of the television tonight, but the guys insisted they go out. For a prime porterhouse cut, he'd give up his planned solitary evening.

"A toast," Luke said, holding up his glass of single malt scotch.

Derek raised his glass and Kade did the same. "What are we toasting to?" he asked.

"To one full week with the same personal assistant. I haven't decided if that means we should be toasting you for your achievement or Lexie for her ability to put up with your shit."

"I'll drink to both," Luke said, treating Kade to a shit-eating grin before tapping Kade's, then Derek's glasses and taking a long sip of his drink.

"Fucking comedians," Kade muttered. The last person he wanted to discuss was Lexie.

Over the delicious meal, they talked about moving forward with their company, careful to avoid discussing Julian and his lawsuit in public. Never knew who might be lurking nearby for a story. Somehow Kade made it through dinner. He didn't want to discuss the fact that he'd struggled to cut the meat, had needed help, and was generally frustrated by too many things at the moment.

He downed the rest of the alcohol in his glass and signaled the waiter, planning to top off his steak with another drink.

"What can I get you?" Andrew, their usual waiter, asked.

"A refill," Kade said, lifting his tumbler. "Macallan 18, neat, filled three-quarters of the way full," he reminded the man. Although he served them every time they came in, Kade left nothing to chance. "I'll also take a fresh bottle of natural spring water, room temperature, and a straw please."

"Of course." The waiter tipped his head discreetly and headed for the bar.

"You're really going to do that straw and water thing again?" Derek asked.

"You know he is, so why bother questioning him?"

Kade shook his head. "Four or five drops of water helps a whiskey—"

"Open up in the glass," Derek and Luke said, repeating his often-used refrain at the same time.

"If you remember, why ask?" Kade posed the rhetorical question.

They did it to give him a hard time as only they could. Because they knew he liked his scotch a certain way, compounded by his need for routine. Only these two men could get away with making fun of him.

The waiter returned and placed Kade's fresh drink, bottle of water, and straw beside his plate.

After the waiter poured the fresh spring water in a glass, Kade used the straw to deposit exactly four drops into his drink. Too much diluted the whiskey. This, at least, he could do without too much help. He'd had an appointment with an orthopedist, who'd merely confirmed the ER doctor's diagnosis and had given him the same talk about not overdoing things. Though he'd said he'd take another look in a month and consider removing the splint then.

Derek placed his napkin on the table. "I'm not ready to go home yet. I heard some people from work say they're hanging at Lights. Want to stop by for a drink?"

Kade hadn't planned on going out late, but he couldn't say heading home alone right now appealed to him either. "Why not?"

"I'm in," Luke said, signaling to the waiter for a check.

"Who's going to be at Lights?" Kade liked to know what he was walking into. "Is that where the coders hang out?"

Luke accepted the folder with the check from the waiter before turning his gaze on Kade. "Actually it's Tessa and Becky," he said, flipping open the billfold.

Kade's stomach twisted at the mention of their personal assistants, who, he'd noticed, Lexie had grown more comfortable with over the course of her first week of work.

He glanced from Luke, who was busy putting the company credit card down, to Derek, who, as usual, had a guilty look on his face.

Don't ask, don't ask, don't ask. "Anyone else?" he asked, hoping that was vague enough to keep his friends from giving him a hard time.

"Let's go find out," Derek said, meeting Kade's gaze with an amused one of his own.

He should have known better than to underestimate his friend and had a feeling he was in for an interesting night.

LEXIE DIDN'T OWN funky clothes, so she borrowed an outfit from her sister. Dressed in a short black leather skirt and red bustier—she figured if she was going out, she was going *all out*—and her own pair of heels, she joined the other women at Lights.

She walked into the club to flashing lights and mirrored walls. All that was missing was a disco ball. Still, with the music flooding around her, her mood lifted even more. Her sister was having dinner with a friend, a guy Lexie knew and liked, so she was here with a clear mind and intended to enjoy it.

She joined Tessa and Becky, who already had a table and were sitting with their drinks. "Hi, ladies."

"You made it!" Becky, wearing a black dress with a deep V and cut-outs on the sides, jumped up from her chair. "Here, sit." She gestured to another seat and Lexie slid into it.

They pulled their chairs closer together, easier to be heard over the loud music.

"Nice outfit," Tessa said, raising her drink in approval. The blonde wore a royal-blue bandage skirt and white cropped top.

"You two look great," Lexie said.

Tessa flipped her long hair off her shoulder. "Thanks! Let's order you a drink. You need to catch up. We're on our second."

The cocktail waitress walked over, and Lexie, who hadn't had alcohol in a good long while, ordered an old standby, an apple martini.

While they waited, they talked about office gossip and other benign subjects, before inevitably the conversation turned. "Any idea how your boss hurt his hand?" Tessa, who Lexie had already determined enjoyed gossip the most, asked.

Lexie blew out a long breath. She'd come out tonight to have fun and not dwell on Kade, the man who frustrated her in two distinctly opposite ways. She wanted to throttle him for the way he was treating her … and she wanted him because he was just too damned sexy for his own good.

It didn't help that she couldn't stop thinking about the more intense, serious parts of Kade, the wistful one when looking at his brother, and the hurt one over an untrue accusation that threatened his entire world. Unfortunately, it was becoming harder to remember the man she could relate to because the jackass seemed to surface more often.

"I heard he was jealous over a woman and slammed his hand into a wall because of her." Becky shrugged. "At least that's what Ava in HR said."

"I heard the same thing, but he's usually so self-contained I just can't see it," Tessa mused.

Becky swirled her drink in the glass. "Do you know anything?" she asked Lexie, who wasn't about to take part in any conversation about her boss.

"Actually I don't."

Becky leaned in closer. "But you took him to the hospital, right?" she pushed, clearly not satisfied with Lexie's reply. "He had to have said *something*."

"Besides *this hurts* and *when the hell will I get taken back*? he didn't say a word." Which was true, as far as their visit to the hospital went.

What happened back at his apartment was an entirely different story and one that would never leave her lips. Not just because she'd signed that damned NDA.

Lexie was loyal. She wouldn't want people gossiping about her that way. And no matter how angry she was at how Kade had handled the situation, she felt for the circumstances in which he now found himself. A rape accusation had to sting. And again, regardless of her frustration with the man, it didn't change her perception about the story he'd told her. The situation had been a grab for cash.

The waitress returned with Lexie's drink, and she gratefully took a long sip. The tart, sweetened liquor slid down her throat and warmed her insides on the way down to her stomach.

Over the next hour, they talked about clothes and makeup, hit on politics, discovered they disagreed and changed the subject, then moved on to where they'd gone to college and other get-to-know-you topics.

Lexie had finished her second drink and agreed to one shot of vodka for good measure, when a good-looking, blonde-haired guy asked her to dance. She had a solid buzz going, was feeling no pain, and loved dancing to the beat of the music. Her partner had good rhythm, a hot, surfer-boy look that any woman would find attractive.

The music tempo grew faster, and her partner stepped in closer, their bodies moving in sync to the rhythm. Between the good high she had from the alcohol and concentrating on moving to the music without missing a beat, she finally had what she'd been looking for tonight. A distraction from thinking about her hot, frustrating boss.

Chapter Six

K ADE WALKED INTO Lights, a nightclub that lived up to its name, and immediately turned around to leave. The glare, heavy strobe lights, and neon flashing were enough to put his anxiety into hyperdrive. He liked things calm and predictable. Between the massive amounts of people and the bursts of light piercing his eyes, he was anything but at ease.

Nothing could make him stick around.

"Lexie's on the dance floor," Luke said, stopping Kade's retreat with a hand on his shoulder.

Except that.

Kade drew a deep breath and turned around, wanting to see Lexie in a different atmosphere than work. Ignoring the triggers around him, he followed Luke through the crowd and toward the center of the club. Music pulsed around him, adding to the feeling of overcrowding in his brain, but he pushed on, expecting to see Lexie with the other women from the office. Instead he found her in the arms of another man.

Kade blinked against the flickering glare of the lights, trying to process the view. Lexie, *his* Lexie and personal assistant, dressed in a black leather skirt that ended mid-thigh and a tight red top with her breasts near to bursting out, moved like a goddess to the music. All rational thought fled from his brain as he watched her gyrate her hips and shake her curves against a surfer dude with wandering hands.

"Go easy," Derek said, standing beside him.

Kade shot him a dirty look. "Would you?"

"When you put it that way, far be it for me to get in the way now that you finally realized what you want."

"Maybe he should say *who*," Luke added, both their voices loud to accommodate the pounding music.

Kade ignored them and strode onto the wooden dance floor, headed straight for Lexie. Just as he reached her, the song changed to one with a faster beat. She squealed in delight, looking up at the ceiling and lifting her arms in the air, swaying to the song.

Before her partner could grab her around the waist, Kade stepped between them.

"Kade!" Lexie exclaimed, her eyes lighting up at the sight of him.

Things had been strained between them all week,

so between the exuberant greeting and the glassy look in her eyes, Kade figured she'd been drinking. Which gave him a legitimate reason to get her off the dance floor and away from this guy.

"Let's go," he said to her.

"Hey!" Surfer Dude folded his arms across his chest, taking a stand. Too bad for him, Kade was bigger, bulkier, and had too much invested to back down easily.

"Casey, meet Kade, my big old mean boss," Lexie said, oblivious to the pissing contest about to take place.

Yep, she was drunk, Kade thought, amused despite himself.

"She's not going anywhere," Surfer Dude informed him.

Lexie looked up at Kade with big blue eyes. "What are you doing here?" she asked, her hips still moving in time to the music, her generous breasts swaying to the beat.

His cock couldn't help responding, and he grew hard in an instant. "I'm taking you home," he informed her.

"Hey." Surfer Dude shoved him hard. "Don't you listen? I said she's—"

"With *me*," Kade said, getting into the guy's personal space. "And don't fucking touch me." He glared at the other man with a look that had most people cowering. One he'd perfected as he'd learned to box and worked out enough to overcome the geekiness of youth. "Now unless you want trouble, as in your teeth all over this floor, walk away now."

"Kade!" Lexie said, outraged.

Casey raised both hands in defeat. "Fine. She's not worth it," he muttered before turning and disappearing into the crowd.

"I lost my dance partner," Lexie said, pouting, her pretty hot pink lips turned downward in a frown.

Kade wanted to seal his mouth over hers and nibble on those plump lips until she opened for him and he could taste her sweetness.

Before he could do just that, she grabbed him around the waist.

"Dance with me!" She moved to the music, her soft body pressed sweetly against his, her belly flush against his now raging erection.

Kade was many things, but a dancer wasn't one of them. The crowds were getting to him. The noise was causing a beat throughout his system that was ramping up his nerves. And the lights made him feel out of control. None of which he liked. All of which had resulted in problems in the past.

He needed to get the hell off the dance floor and find a quiet corner to calm the fuck down. He needed to be alone with Lexie.

"Come on." He grabbed her hand and pulled her along with him, off the wooden floor, past Derek and Luke, who'd gotten themselves drinks and had been enjoying the show he put on.

He continued on beyond the crowded bar to a hallway that had a line of people waiting for the restrooms. Shit. A big red EXIT sign beckoned at the far end, and when he reached it, the door was propped open with a milk crate, letting fresh air into the packed area.

"Thank God," he muttered.

"Where are we going?" she asked, pressing herself up against his back, whether on purpose or because of the many people, he didn't know or care.

"Outside for air," he said over his shoulder. Never letting go of her hand, he stepped outside and walked down a small alley until the music faded enough for him to be able to hear again, which, in turn, enabled him to start to calm down.

"Oh, it feels good out here," Lexie said. Lifting her long hair up, she leaned forward, letting air blow against her damp neck. "Whew!" She shook out her hair, which had the effect of wriggling her ass.

Kade let out a low groan. The woman was going to be the death of him. He leaned against the brick façade of a building and took in the cool night air. Closing his eyes, he breathed in and out slowly, counting upward by four and down by four, until his heart rate slowed to a comfortable beat.

He opened his eyes to find Lexie staring at him in silence. Her makeup had smudged beneath her eyes, and she'd twisted her hair back into some sort of messy knot, but she'd never looked more beautiful.

"Are you okay?" she asked, that perceptiveness he loved about her returning now that they'd had a few minutes of quiet.

"I am now."

She stepped closer. "Why, Kade?"

He figured she was asking why he was here. "Luke and Derek wanted to come out after dinner."

She shook her head. "No, why not just leave me alone? You could be having drinks with your friends, but instead you're interrupting my night. *Why?*"

She'd inched into his personal space, was pushing for answers he didn't want to face, let alone give.

Her luscious breasts were rising and falling, so close he could reach out and touch. Her scent permeated the space around them, a fragrance he couldn't get out of his head or his dreams.

"Tell me what you want," she said, frustration tingeing her tone.

Frustration he felt as well. "I. Want. You." No sooner had he said the words than she launched herself against him, and his mouth came down hard on hers.

He expected her to fight him, but she gave in willingly, her lips softening beneath his, and suddenly Kade had everything he wanted at his fingertips. The churning he'd been experiencing inside himself ever since Julian had targeted him and he'd deliberately pushed Lexie away faded into the background. Gone because she was in his arms.

He slid his mouth back and forth, devouring the lips he'd been so focused on earlier, nibbling, tasting, sliding his tongue deep inside. She moaned, meeting him halfway, tongues tangling, breath mingling, bodies grinding against each other as if they couldn't get enough.

God knew Kade couldn't. He broke the kiss long enough to give her instructions. "Jump up. Wrap your legs around my waist."

She pushed her skirt up and complied with his request. He pulled her roughly against him, turning them so it was her back against the wall, his body thrusting against hers, grinding into her until she was panting and groaning in his arms. He wanted to bare her sweet pussy to his gaze, slide his fingers over her slick lips, and coat his fingers in her wetness.

She rotated her hips against him, her feminine heat pulsing against that hard-as-stone part of his body. He clenched his jaw, needing so much more. He wanted to take her hard, fast, and *now*. But he retained enough awareness to know where they were, what they could and couldn't do. He also knew she deserved more than an outside fuck against the wall of some club. Even if they were simulating the act now, her hips rotating around and around, his body thrusting against hers.

Which meant this impulsive night had to come to an end.

He was about to lower her to the ground when she arched her back and let out a shuddering moan. "Close, Kade. I'm so close."

He gritted his teeth and wondered what the fuck to do. As her boss, he couldn't screw her and face her afterwards as if it meant nothing. As if *she* meant nothing. And he still owed her an apology for how badly he'd treated her almost from the beginning. Kade didn't apologize to anyone. He'd spent his childhood doing too damned much of that to his mother. But he'd damn well do it for Lexie. Then he'd consider fucking her, like he wanted to.

"Please, Kade. Make me come." Lexie was so far gone she trembled in his arms. He couldn't leave her hanging on the edge like this either.

He slipped his hand beneath her skirt, coming into contact with a barely there, soaking wet thong. Jesus, he thought, this was the ultimate test of restraint. He slid his fingers over her slick lips and found her clit, rubbing with his thumb.

Her thighs tightened around his hips, and she buried her face in the crook of his neck, riding his hand as he worked one long finger inside her. Her orgasm hit immediately, and she rocked against him, her tight body clasping around him. Leaving him to imagine it wasn't his finger but his cock that she was milking dry.

He pressed his thumb hard against her clit, letting her ride out her climax until she was spent. He held her afterwards, his hard body protesting every second.

Eventually she relaxed in his arms, and he removed his hand, slid her down, helping her fix her skirt and shift her tight top until she was comfortable.

"I don't…"

He placed a finger over her lips. The same finger he'd had inside her seconds before. "Don't. We both needed this."

"But you didn't—"

"I got what I needed for now," he assured her, even if his aching dick disagreed.

She nodded, her cheeks flushed, her hair in complete disarray. She was flustered and so fucking sweet he wanted to devour her all over again.

"Let me take you home," he said, needing to see her safe.

"But what about Tessa and Becky?" she asked.

"Won't they wonder what happened to me?"

"I guarantee you, Derek and Luke will explain." Just like he'd have to deal with their shit come morning.

But, Kade thought, thinking back on the last few minutes, he could take whatever they dished out. Because the time with Lexie had been so fucking worth it.

LEXIE WOKE UP to a pounding headache and a mixed bag of memories from the night before. What the hell had she been thinking, letting Kade take her outside, climbing him like a jungle gym and… Oh my God, she didn't want to remember any more. Except her body tingled in all the right places, her sex completely on board with what had happened last night.

She turned and buried her face in the pillow. How was she ever going to face him on Monday? At least he'd told her there was no dry cleaning this weekend so she didn't have to face him today.

Before she could dwell on that awful possibility, she heard a knock on her bedroom door. Time to face her sister. "Come in!"

Her twin walked in carrying a cup of coffee and set it down on the nightstand. "I heard you come in late last night. I thought you could use a pick-me-up."

"Bless you," Lexie said, surprised her sister was being so sweet to her. Lately things had been strained.

Kendall sat down beside her in bed, curling her legs beneath her. "Did you go out and have fun?"

Lexie felt her cheeks burn at the innocent question. "I was with two girls from work. We went to a nightclub and ... yeah, I had fun." More than she'd had in a while.

If she took Kade and the fact that she'd begged him to make her come out of the equation, she'd acted more her age than she'd been able to in years.

Of course, she couldn't take Kade out of the equation because she thought about him constantly. She'd been drunk early in the evening, but by the time he'd arrived, she'd just been high on life and enjoying herself. When she'd asked him to dance, she'd been trying to get him to do the same. And, of course, to break up the tension from his confrontation with Casey, her dance partner, who she hadn't been interested in, but he did have the moves and she'd wanted to dance.

But Kade hadn't been comfortable in the club, something she'd realized too late. He'd been uptight and had barreled for an exit like a man possessed. Once outside, the relief on his face had been apparent. There was more to Kaden Barnes than she could put her finger on. More that she wanted to understand, but after her brazen behavior, she doubted she'd be around long enough to find out anything more.

"What's wrong?" Kendall asked, watching her over her mug as she took a sip of coffee. "You look worried."

Lexie narrowed her gaze at her sister's concern. Not that it wasn't in character. Deep down, Kendall was a good soul. She just had issues that often took over. Which was why Lexie cherished the times Kendall was ... Kendall. Her sweet, caring, fun-loving twin.

Lexie leaned her head back and met Kendall's gaze. "I'm thinking about my boss. He's ... different."

"Good different?"

"Sexy different," she admitted. "But he's also difficult and demanding and he's my *boss*. You don't mix business with pleasure and still have a job the next day."

"Is that what you did?" Kendall placed the mug on the nightstand and moved in closer. "Did you sleep with your boss?"

"No!" Lexie was quick to dispel that thought, and she wasn't going to elaborate on what she had done with Kade.

"You just want to. Got it. What does he look like?" her sister asked.

"His name is Kaden Barnes, and he's been in the

news for his app, Blink. You can Google him later."

"Oh, I've heard of him! He's rich. Wouldn't it be nice not to have to think about money?" Kendall said wistfully.

Lexie rolled her eyes. "It's not like we're exactly hurting. We have parents who make sure we don't starve." It was on the tip of Lexie's tongue to ask about the shopping bags she'd seen in Kendall's room. And to bug her about getting at least a part-time job, something that let her put one foot back into the real world. But that would cause an argument, and she'd lose the peaceful calm she was experiencing now.

"Do you want to go out for pancakes?" Kendall asked, unaware of Lexie's thoughts. "I have a craving for them."

As if in reply, Lexie's stomach growled, and she laughed at the timing. "Let me jump into the shower and I'll be ready soon," she said instead of picking a fight by putting Kendall on the defensive with intrusive questions.

Lexie followed her heart, not her gut, and decided to cherish this precious time with the sister she loved during one of her more stable moments.

After a weekend to dwell on the fact that she'd begged Kade to make her come, she showed up at work and waited for him to arrive. Her sister had gone out with a friend again Saturday night, and she was looking for a job in retail, giving Lexie even more hope she was making progress. Add in the medicine change, which would kick in soon, and possibilities were endless. She couldn't even bring herself to temper her expectations this time. She was too invested in things going right for once.

She sat at her desk, her eyes and ears primed for the old elevator, when Becky walked over to her desk. "Hey! Are you feeling better?" she asked.

Lexie wrinkled her nose in confusion. "Why do you ask?"

"Derek said you weren't feeling well and Kade made sure you got home safely."

Oh. "Oh! Yes, I'd … had a lot to drink and I was dizzy. Kade took me outside for fresh air—" And an orgasm. "And then he had his driver take me home. I felt much better the next day. I'm sorry if I worried you, but I really did have a great time with you and Tessa."

"Oh, good." Relief flooded the other woman's expression. "I had fun too. We'll have to do it again soon."

"I'd like that," Lexie said. Before she could speak further, the elevator mechanism sounded, and it beeped loudly when reaching their floor. She popped up from her seat. "Coffee calls!"

Becky shook her head, her red hair falling over one

shoulder. "Your boss is a slave driver. I don't think I could deal with the demands," she said, keeping Lexie company as she walked to the Keurig.

"I don't mind," she said honestly. The coffee was the easy part of her job. Facing him today was going to be the most difficult.

Becky shrugged. "Well, I've got to get back. I'll talk to you later." She smiled at Lexie before turning and heading across the floor to her desk.

Lexie finished stirring the two sugars into the coffee, drew a deep breath, and forced her legs to move toward Kade's office, unable to cross the threshold. She stood in the doorway, observing him unnoticed.

Thanks to his splint, he couldn't shave, and he'd grown a healthy beard. Instead of hiding his handsome face, the scruff defined his features, giving him an even edgier appearance. Her sex, already primed by him on Friday night, tingled at the sight of his raw masculinity.

Her high school/college boyfriend had been just that, a boy, in comparison to Kade, her feelings juvenile in contrast to the overwhelmingly female, adult sensations and emotions Kade inspired in her. But she didn't have time to dwell on those differences now. Not here.

She shook her head, reminding herself she was at work and needed to do her job. And to do that, she had to put their night behind them.

"Good morning," she said in an effort to capture his attention.

He jerked his head up and met her gaze, his green eyes almost emerald this morning, and they brightened at the sight of her. That was a first, but she'd be lying if she said the heat in his gaze didn't thrill her.

"Lexie," he said, his voice rough, as if he hadn't yet used it today.

"I have your coffee," she said stupidly, because why else would she be standing in the doorway with a mug in her hand?

"Come in."

She stepped into the room, pretending just looking at him didn't have her stomach doing back flips.

"I thought about you this weekend. Wondered how you were feeling." He tipped his head, studying her.

She could say she was fine and let things go or choose the more difficult path and get the awkwardness out of the way by being up front.

She placed his coffee onto the desk and forced herself to meet his gaze again. "You mean was I hungover after my big night out? Or did I spend the weekend mortified that I jumped my boss in a back alley?" she asked, being up front and honest. Because Lexie always had to choose the tougher path.

An amused bark of laughter escaped his throat. "And here I thought you'd try to avoid me this morning," he said, admiration in his gaze.

"Well, cowering isn't my style." She clasped her hands together in front of her, doing her best not to fidget. "I figured I should give you the opportunity to fire me if you want to. I know you said you wouldn't, but Friday night was completely inappropriate and—"

"One hundred percent mutual," he informed her, taking her off guard, as did the suddenly sexy smile on his lips.

She rocked back on her heels, nearly losing her footing in surprise. "Kade."

"I'm not firing you. You keep me on my toes, and that's not an easy feat."

He had her on *her* toes now, completely off-kilter and aware from the look in his eyes that something between them had changed. And that something both drew her in and made her wary at the same time.

Especially when he continued to stare at her, devouring her as if he hadn't had a meal all weekend. And considering he hadn't kissed her since Friday night, maybe he hadn't.

She shivered at the so-very-sinful path her thoughts had taken. He was her boss. The man whose moods changed on a whim. And he hadn't broken eye contact, which had her entire body lighting up with desire only he managed to ignite inside her.

Wrong. It was so very wrong. Which didn't stop her from wanting him badly.

Chapter Seven

KADE STARED INTO Lexie's wary blue eyes and knew he should take heed of the warning there. She wasn't all in. She was obviously confused by what had transpired between them.

He wasn't.

He'd had a long weekend to think, and he hadn't been able to concentrate on anything except Lexie and what she'd felt like coming apart—around his finger and in his arms. She invaded every conscious and unconscious thought he'd had. He'd even dreamed about sliding his cock inside her and finding heaven in her slick, warm, wet pussy.

The more rational part of him knew he shouldn't have let things go as far as they had on Friday night, but he hadn't been able to resist. The sexy woman at the club had revealed another facet to the able assistant who had no trouble going toe-to-toe with him by day. Her confidence and fearlessness, at least when it came to dealing with him, was refreshing, and it turned him on.

Everything about her turned him on.

She was different from the women in his past—from her honesty to her caring nature, Lexie was unique. Yet he couldn't allow himself to believe it would last.

He had his past breathing down his neck, a reminder of what kind of betrayal the females in his life brought him and a threat to his future. As a result, he'd tried to convince himself that getting involved with Lexie further wasn't a good idea.

None of which stopped him from both thinking about her constantly and deciding it was time to do something about it. Which was what he planned to do now.

She watched him from beneath hooded eyes, waiting for him to make a move, and he did. He strode determinedly around his desk and came up beside her, her sweet scent a reminder of that endless kiss in the alley. The combination of tart, like her personality, and sweet, like her taste, just did it for him.

He stepped closer, forcing her to look up at him despite her sexy-as-sin heels.

"You're not firing me?" she asked, breaking into his wicked thoughts.

He smiled, something that seemed to come easier around her. "No, I'm not firing you."

"Then what *are* you doing with me?"

"This." He hooked an arm around her waist, pulled her close, and sealed his lips over hers.

She stilled, her hands coming to rest on his shoulders, and like the other night, he braced himself for a hard shove. Instead she curled her fingers into his shirt and kissed him back, her tongue gliding over his lips delicately in a sweet caress.

He groaned, nipping her lower lip until she parted and let him inside. He swept through the luscious depths of her mouth, losing himself in her sweetness. His tongue tangled with hers, thrusting in and out, drinking in her shuddering moans.

He wanted more. Needed to possess her. He grasped the back of her neck with his good hand, buried his fingers in her thick hair, and tilted her head for deeper access, sliding his tongue farther inside, getting more demanding with every sweep.

Her nails dug through his shirt, into his skin, arousing him beyond belief. He backed her against the desk, until her ass settled on the metal surface. Then, removing his hand from her hair, he slid his fingers up her silk blouse until he cupped her breast in his palm, her hardened nipple pressing against him.

His heartbeat sped up at the feel of the tight peak

pressing hard into his skin. Never had he felt anything so good, and he'd yet to touch her bare flesh. He glided his lips down her jaw, pressing wet kisses to the pulse below her ear, using the time to breathe in and gather his wits, which had long since disappeared.

"This is wrong," she whispered, causing him to realize he'd given her time to think too. But the words were coming out breathy and soft, her need obvious. "I work for you."

"There's no office policy preventing it," he said, grabbing on to any rational reason to keep her right where she was.

He liked the feel of the lace covering of her bra against his hand. It let him imagine what her actual flesh would feel like to the touch. He wondered if her nipples would taste as sweet as her mouth.

"Kade, this is insane."

"Agreed." He swallowed hard against the pulse pounding in his temples.

She was right. It wasn't a smart move. He wasn't completely sure he'd ever trust any woman completely, but he couldn't not pursue her. Couldn't let her go.

"But it's still happening," he informed her, bound and determined to have his way. If she really didn't want to be with him, he'd walk in a heartbeat.

He'd never forced himself on a woman. Never would, no matter what Lila had claimed. But this pliant, sexy female in his arms wasn't saying no, and he had every intention of seducing her further.

Not here and now, but in the very near future.

He plucked her nipple between his thumb and forefinger, rolling it between the pads of his fingers. "We're good together."

A full-body tremor shook her, and she whimpered, the sound going straight to his dick.

"But, Kade, I need this job." She pushed him with both hands, and he stepped back immediately.

"I respect that." He met her gaze, trying his damnedest not to look at her puffy lips, red and swollen from his heated kisses. "Nothing that happens between us will affect your work here," he promised her.

She raised her eyebrows in disbelief. "That's naïve, and the one thing you, Kaden Barnes, are not is naïve."

"No, I'm determined." To have her in his bed and in his office.

In the short time they'd been together, she'd been a model assistant, despite him being an obnoxious ass. Her predecessors had walked out sooner with less provocation. He intended to keep Lexie happy on all levels.

She sighed, folding her arms across her chest, a move obviously designed to hide her full breasts and prevent him from staring. He glanced down, but that view didn't help, her sexy skirt not a deterrent to the places his mind wanted to travel, and reminded him of when he'd slid his fingers up her tight skirt and played her body until she came. Hard.

He forced himself to refocus on her objections and ways around them. "When … if … things between us end, you'll have a choice whether to continue working for me or move to another position here. Same salary, same benefits, no hassle from me," he promised.

Not that he could imagine her leaving his employ. Or him.

"Make no mistake, no matter what, I intend to pursue you, Lexie. To make it difficult, if not impossible, for you to walk away." He swept his hand through her hair, tugging as he pulled his fingers through the long strands. "So?"

She looked up at him with wide blue eyes. "You're a hard man to say no to," she murmured.

He felt himself grin. "That's what I was hoping you'd say."

"So what's next? We get to work?" She hopped off the desk and began adjusting her clothes, her cheeks pink and adorably on fire.

"We do, but one more thing. There's a benefit I have to attend Saturday night, and I don't want to go alone. Blink is a major donor, and I'm doing the representing at this particular gala."

He and his partners took turns at various charitable events. Kade never brought a date and had shocked himself by asking Lexie now. But he was coming to realize that his feelings for her were stronger than the internal battle he fought with himself over letting someone in.

"What is the benefit for?" she asked.

"MHA of NYC," he said, bracing for what she'd ask next.

"What does it stand for?"

"Mental Health Association of New York City."

She sucked in a startled breath. "Is this coincidence? Me telling you about my mother and you asking me to attend a benefit for mental health?"

"It is." They had more in common than she realized. Maybe not the same classification of issues, but they each understood mental health better than the average person.

"It's also a cause that means something to me," he said, leaving it at that. He wasn't ready to share his reasons with her. He might not ever be ready. "I'll pick you up at eight Saturday night."

She blinked up at him. "You're moving awfully fast."

"I always do when I want something." And he'd decided he wanted her. "Do we have an understanding?"

She ran her tongue over her lips, and he hoped like hell she was tasting him, because he sure as hell still savored her.

"We have an understanding," she said at last, allowing Kade to breathe easy for the first time since she'd walked into the room.

LEXIE KNEW HOW to live in the moment. It was the only way she could get through life as she knew it. So she put Saturday night out of her head and went about her week, planning to keep things business as usual. Except there was nothing usual as Kade stepped up his game.

Tuesday morning, he brought her a hot cup of Starbucks, handing it to her at the same time she brought his coffee into his office.

"Thank you," she said, surprised as she accepted the white cup with green writing.

He watched, a hopeful look in his green eyes as she took a careful sip of the hot brew, sampling the extremely sugary drink. "Mmm. What is this?" she asked, licking her lips for another taste.

"White chocolate mocha latte with whipped cream. You like it?"

"It's delicious. How did you choose the flavor?"

A pleased grin lifted his sexy lips. "Because it's sweet. Like you." He crooked a finger, silently beckoning her to join him.

She couldn't resist and slowly made her way around the desk, swaying her hips as she walked over. His darkening gaze let her know he hadn't missed the deliberate show. She stopped close to him and inhaled his potent masculine scent.

"Thank me," he instructed.

"I already did." And she didn't appreciate being told to do so.

"The right way. The way you would if we weren't in the office."

She narrowed her gaze, admittedly confused. "I don't understand."

"Kiss me," he said, elaborating more fully.

She blinked in surprise and had no doubt he didn't think she'd comply. Not here, with his office door open.

Normally he'd be right. But he'd thrown down a challenge, and Lexie never passed up a challenge. Besides, he looked delectable in his black track pants and light blue Trekkie tee shirt.

So she rose onto her tiptoes and pressed her mouth against his. With a groan, he looped an arm around her waist and pulled her closer. Her feet practically dangled off the floor as he swept his tongue inside and took control. He devoured her, and she loved how he tilted her head so he could kiss her more deeply, take more from her. He had a talented mouth and tongue, and kissing Kade was definitely becoming her favorite kind of foreplay.

She had no doubt this was a prelude to whatever he ultimately had planned. He'd said he intended to pursue her, and he did just that, seducing her with his mouth until her toes curled and she fell forward in her heels.

He grasped her harder to keep her upright and pulled his head back. She stared into his eyes, hazy with desire.

"Any more commands?" she asked, catching her breath.

"Give me some time to come to myself, and I'm sure I'll think of something." A dimple she hadn't noticed before appeared in his cheek, and she realized she'd do anything to see it again.

For the rest of the week, he continued his Starbucks gifts. True, he still expected his coffee made his way—he was Kaden Barnes, after all, and she wouldn't want him any other way. He didn't kiss her again at the office, but he did touch her more.

A caress on the cheek.

A tug on her hair.

An ass grab when they were alone.

Somehow they fell into a routine. She rearranged his desk again, this time so he could use the mouse and laptop easier with his left hand. She took notes for him in meetings with investors, learned more of what went on in his business, and discovered she also enjoyed his favorite lunch, grilled chicken on whole wheat bread, mayonnaise, and two slices of avocado. He noticed when there was only one slice of the green fruit.

On Friday, she walked into the office after he'd taken what sounded like a heated phone call and caught him shaking a pill from a prescription bottle into his hand. Everything in her wanted to ask … but she didn't. He knew she'd seen him.

If he wanted her to know, he'd explain. Instead he snapped at her. "Can you fucking knock before you just walk in?"

"The door was open," she reminded him. "Anyone could have walked in. If you're looking for privacy, I suggest you be more careful." She turned and walked out.

He avoided her for the rest of the day, leaving early without explanation. But a deliveryman came by with a lily of the valley plant.

How did she know? A plastic card was stuck between the leaves with the explanation: *Lily of the Valley—symbolizes a return to happiness. This plant must be treated with care just like the relationship in which you and the recipient are engaged.*

The note from Kade was much more down-to-earth. *I'm an ass and I'm sorry. Kade.* She'd smiled the whole way home.

After work, she and Kendall took the train to their parents' house. They were overdue for a visit, and Lexie needed to pick up a dress to wear on Saturday night. Their apartment was small, and she'd had no need to keep anything formal there.

Kendall had offered to come with her, and Lexie gratefully agreed. She'd rather visit home with her twin than alone. For all her issues, she and Kendall had their mother in common, and it was easier to deal with her with someone by her side.

They sat side by side on the train with Waffles in a pet carrier, when Kendall took her by surprise. "I met someone," her sister said.

Lexie whipped her head around and looked at her sister, whose cheeks were flushed a healthy pink. She stared at Lexie, waiting for a response.

"Where?"

"At the gym. I was getting off the elliptical, and this cute guy walked over and asked if I wanted to grab a shake at the snack area. We talked for an hour and had so much in common." Kendall turned, one elbow on the top of the seat back behind her. "We're going out on Saturday night."

"Oh! What's his name? What does he do for a living? How do you know he's … I don't know, safe?" All the immediate questions floating in her brain spewed out of her mouth before she could censor herself.

"Could you just be happy for me for once instead of hounding me and questioning my judgment?" Kendall snapped.

Lexie blew out a long breath. "You're right. I just… I worry."

Was it smart for her sister to be going out on a date with a guy she'd just met? Was she in a place where she could pick out the good from the sleazy? Lexie curled her fingers into a fist but said nothing.

Kendall tucked a leg beneath her. "Fine. His name is Jay, and he's in the middle of complicated negotiations with his partners in some company. I can't remember the name. Anyway, until they work things out, he has free time on his hands, so he was at the gym during the day." Kendall met her gaze. "He said I have pretty eyes," she whispered, a dorky smile on her face.

No doubt about it, her sister was smitten. "You know I just want what's best for you, right?"

"I do and I love you for it. Trust me, Jay's a nice guy."

Lexie hoped so. Before she could respond, a voice announced their stop. "This is us. Ready?" she asked, pushing herself to a standing position.

"To visit the old homestead? Sure thing." They shared a knowing gaze, neither one of them wanting to address the sad truth.

Nobody knew what to expect from Addy Parker. Although their father knew they were coming, not even Wade knew what mood his wife would be in at any given time.

"MY GIRLS!" WADE Parker hugged Kendall and Lexie in turn and in no particular order.

"It's so good to be home," Kendall said, letting Waffles out of his carrier. The dog immediately ran to Wade, jumping up and down for attention, which their father immediately gave. They'd already walked the dog after getting off the train, so Waffles was good to tag along with Kendall toward the kitchen.

Lexie glanced toward the curved staircase in the center hall colonial leading up to the master bedroom suite. No sounds came from above, and she wondered if her mother was in a darkened room or downstairs somewhere. Her father's silence on the subject didn't bode well.

She picked up her pace, joining her sister and dad

as they reached the kitchen. The room had been remodeled since she'd grown up here, but more so her father could keep the house current and up to date than because her mother needed a place to cook. Tonight her father had dinner waiting. He'd brought in from a local restaurant that they'd favored growing up. Which meant her mother was definitely incapacitated.

With a sigh, she pasted a smile on her face and talked with her father about his work as an investment banker, which eventually turned to him questioning Lexie about her new job.

"So how's the working world?" he asked as they sat around the table, eating chicken Marsala.

Lexie smiled. "I'm enjoying it."

"Barnes isn't making you crazy? I admit when Derek said he was the one who needed an assistant, I was worried. The boy's got his quirks."

"Really, Dad? Glass houses and all that. Who are we to judge anyone else?" she asked, immediately jumping to Kade's defense.

"Whoa. I didn't mean anything except facts. He's difficult…"

"Demanding with good reason."

"Obstinate—"

"Stubborn."

"Peculiar."

"He has idiosyncrasies." Like anxiety and ADHD

121

he tried to keep hidden.

From how he aligned the pens on his desk *any time they got out of order* to his fresh coffee, to the precise way his shirts were lined up in his closet—this she knew because she'd brought his dry cleaning to his apartment and had to hang them up. She'd taken the time to undo the plastic and put the clean shirts at exactly the same width apart like the others before leaving things just as she'd found them.

"Quirks," she added. Adorable quirks, Lexie thought.

"Protective much?" Kendall asked, putting down her fork and staring at her sister. "Someone has a thing for her boss!"

Her father's fork clattered to the table. "You do?"

"Would you both cool it?" Lexie said, her face flaming.

"She needs to pick up a dress for a formal event Saturday night. With her boss." Kendall waggled her eyebrows.

Lexie shot her sister an annoyed glare. "It's a business affair."

"At least she admits it's an affair." Kendall laughed, the sound musical to Lexie's ears. Especially when they were in this house, where laughter and true happiness were rare.

Ignoring the innuendo, Lexie decided to address

the elephant in the room. "Where's Mom?"

"She's under the weather," Wade said, using his old fallback excuse.

"You mean she's upstairs in your bedroom, shades drawn, hiding under the covers," Kendall muttered.

"Actually she's sitting in the rocker," he said, picking up his plate and heading for the sink.

The rocker was worse than the bed. If Lexie closed her eyes, she could hear the creak of the old chair as her mother pushed back and forth in an endless cycle.

"God, why can't the doctors do something for her?" Kendall asked. Frustrated, she shoved back her chair and began cleaning the table with her father.

Although Lexie knew she should help, she quietly left the room and made her way upstairs, her stomach in knots. She walked slowly down the hall and pushed open the double doors to her parents' bedroom, hearing the creak of the chair before she set foot inside.

"Mom?" Lexie asked into the dark room.

No reply.

She walked farther in and sat on the edge of the bed, on her father's side, while her mother rocked in the chair. "Mom, it's Lexie."

More creaking noises from the chair.

Lexie curled her legs beneath her and sighed, as frustrated as Kendall that they no longer had their mother around. Over the years, they'd had less and less of Addy and more of … this.

She wanted to be able to tell her mom about Kade, just like she'd wanted to talk to her when she'd lost her virginity after her prom and decided she was really in love with John. But her mom had been *under the weather*, and her father hadn't wanted her disturbed.

"I'm falling for my boss," Lexie said out loud, just to see if she could get a rise from her mother.

Nothing.

With a lump in her throat and the same old lead weight on her chest, she rose to her feet and walked out of the room.

With Kendall, no matter how bad things got, there was a flicker, a spark of personality, someone and something to fight for. Her mother was long gone, and Lexie feared her father hadn't faced that fact yet. When he did, he'd have to consider putting her in a home where she could get more specialized care—and he could go on with his life. If such a thing were possible.

She walked back downstairs, not wanting to draw attention to where she'd been or argue with her father about upsetting her mother. He was so overprotective of her it wasn't an easy balance for Lexie to deal with.

As she approached the kitchen again, she heard the sound of raised voices, her father and sister, arguing.

"I said no. I already gave you money to buy interview clothes. I can't imagine you need more." Their father rarely raised his voice, so Lexie assumed this conversation had been going on since she'd walked out.

"Dad, please. It'll be the last time. I promise. I just really need—"

"What?" Lexie asked. "You really need what?" She stepped into the room.

"Nothing. It's between me and Dad."

"Of course it is," Lexie muttered.

Lexie glanced at her father, who guiltily looked away. Well, at least the shopping bags had an explanation; however, she doubted her sister had been buying *interview clothes*.

When they both remained quiet, Lexie threw her hands up in frustration. She headed to the table only to discover they'd already cleaned up.

"Your rooms are available if you want to stay over," her father said as if nothing was wrong.

Which was the story of her life. Sweep everything under the rug and pretend. "No, I think I'll pick up what I need and head back to the city."

Kendall pouted. "Well, I think I'll stay."

Probably to spend more time pressuring their dad for cash. Lexie shrugged, fed up with all of it. "Suit yourself."

Feeling suffocated by this house, the people in it, and the painful memories, she needed to get out of here.

A little while later, the dress she'd worn to her father's big formal company Christmas party was packed up. She added a pair of sexy heels and dressy jewelry she didn't normally need and headed back to the city.

Alone.

Lexie stepped off the train at Penn Station after dark and decided to splurge on a taxi instead of taking the subway uptown by herself. Depressed from seeing her mother, and particularly down after getting confirmation that her sister's excessive spending wasn't under control, which meant her illness wasn't either, Lexie's emotions were at the surface.

She felt raw, fragile, and alone. The only person she could turn to for understanding was her father, and clearly he was having his own challenges dealing with her mom and sister. Sometimes she was angry with him for keeping her mother at home, for not trying harder, for giving Kendall money ... and other times she felt sorry for him because in addition to a full-time job, he had to juggle his wife's and his daughter's problems.

It wasn't like she thought she could do a better job. Hell, Kendall lived under Lexie's roof, and she couldn't keep track of what her sister did when Lexie wasn't around.

She really didn't want to go home to the empty apartment, where she'd do nothing but dwell on her frustrations and worry about her family. Waffles wouldn't even be there to greet and distract her, but she had no choice. The only person she wanted to be with, to talk to, was someone she wasn't close enough to warrant calling ... just because she needed a friend or an ear. But she still had to fight the urge to give the driver Kade's address, because she believed he'd understand her sadness and frustration.

Which was odd, considering they were just beginning to test the idea of a relationship outside the office. Because she still was worried about mixing business and pleasure. And because she just knew her personal life, her sister, mother, father were all ticking time bombs waiting to explode and drag her under, ruining everything in her life she cared about. Including Kade, should she let him near.

After a difficult night's sleep and a lot of tossing and turning, Lexie woke up Saturday morning, an entire day of beauty appointments ahead of her. Although it was hard, she had no choice but to put last night behind her and focus on today. She'd splurged on a spa day. She had appointments for a massage, manicure, pedicure, spray tan, waxing, and hair before having her makeup professionally done at Saks Fifth

Avenue.

By the time she returned home to get dressed, she felt like a princess, never having treated herself quite this way before. To her relief, her sister wasn't home when she returned. Of course, she experienced a healthy dose of guilt, as well, for feeling that way. Waffles was nowhere to be found, so maybe her twin was still at her parents' place.

No matter, Lexie had a date to finish getting ready for and a man she couldn't wait to see.

Chapter Eight

SATURDAY NIGHT WITH Lexie felt like it was weeks away instead of only one night. Kade's mind whirled with all the problems he was worried about, and instead of focusing on his upcoming date, he obsessed about Julian's vendetta. At times like this, he missed his regular workouts, where he could count out reps, one soothing number after the other. But thanks to his damned hand, he was sidelined. Lifting weights didn't just bulk up his muscles, it calmed him during times of stress, and he had a lot of tension to work out. So he'd turned to the treadmill, but he had a hard time quieting his brain. And he ended up running … and dwelling—fuck, he was *obsessing*—about his one-time friend and his threat to Kade and his company.

So far, the investigator his partners had hired had come up empty on anything about Julian's current life to use against him. According to the PI, Julian was currently clean, working the program ... and coming after Blink's money. The guy was digging deeper into Julian's recent past. Unless they came up with something to counter his ex-friend's threats, they'd have to pay him big money for his minimal role in Blink and to keep quiet, something Kade wasn't willing to do. All of which left him antsy and out of control.

Kade didn't like when life wasn't manageable. Orderly. Under his direct command. As a young kid, he'd thrown tantrums and acted out when he felt frazzled and overwhelmed, which resulted in his father soothing him with *things*. Whatever money could buy. As an adult, Kade had developed subtler techniques to handle his emotions and anxiety.

Upon entering college, he'd been unwilling to admit he needed help, instead trying to tackle his issues himself. He'd minored in psychology in a search for answers, and his studies had allowed him to accept that he had difficulties that necessitated therapy and medication. Too bad his parents hadn't taken the time to figure that out when he was younger, but there was no point dwelling on the past now.

Derek and Luke joined him at the gym Saturday morning, where he ran hard, and they talked about everything but Julian and their potential business problem. His friends understood they were helping Kade work out his stress, and they needed to do the same. They might have his back, but their futures were at stake too.

The one bright spot in his day was an event he might otherwise find a reason to bail on and cut a nice check instead. He supported the MHA without reservation, but he wasn't in the mood to socialize with people. He was, however, in the mood to spend the night with Lexie.

He hired a car for the night, dressed in the tuxedo he tried to wear as little as possible in any given calendar year, and gave the driver Lexie's address.

He'd planned to pick her up at her apartment door but instead found her waiting downstairs at exactly the time he said he'd arrive.

She was dressed in a white dress with an off-the-shoulder contrasting black band; the hem fell high in the front, revealing her gorgeously tanned legs and black sandal heels. The dress skimmed her luscious, mouth-watering curves. And her hair fell over her shoulder in long curls, making his fingers itch to wrap themselves around the long strands and tug while he kissed her bright red mouth.

She took his breath away. Every long minute he'd waited to see her this weekend had been worth it, and as he climbed out of the car to greet her, a single red rose in his good hand, he needed a second to steady his breathing and calm his sudden, burning need.

"Lexie," he said, walking up to her. She glanced up at him and smiled. "You look gorgeous."

A pretty blush stained her cheeks. "Thank you." She reached up and straightened his bow tie. "You dress up nicely yourself."

She slid her hand down his lapel, and it was all he could do not to grab her small wrist, pull her against him, and let her feel the depths of his desire.

He extended the rose, the same color as her lips, the flower the only means he could come up with to convey he was glad she'd agreed to join him.

"Thank you. It's beautiful."

"Not as exquisite as you." He couldn't stop the compliments, and when she smiled radiantly, he didn't want to. "Are you ready to go?" he asked in a roughened voice.

She nodded.

He held out a hand, and she placed her palm against his. A shock of electricity raced through him at that simple touch, and he curled his fingers possessively around hers, leading her to the open car door. He helped her into the backseat.

The driver sped away from the curb, and he studied this beautiful woman sitting next to him in charged silence. Her makeup was heavier than usual, thick lashes fluttering over big blue eyes, her soft, pillowy lips beckoning to him.

"How was your weekend?" he finally managed to ask.

She turned toward him and paused before answering. "Not so great, to be honest."

"I'm a good listener." He offered her an ear because he was truly interested in her life.

"It's just... I went home last night to pick up my dress. And my mother was holed up in her room, unresponsive. Completely unaware that I was even in the room. I was shattered, but my sister didn't seem to be affected at all." She shook her head, her eyes shimmering with tears. "Forget it. I don't want to ruin our night by starting it on a down note." She turned her head, glancing out the window.

"Hey. Don't apologize or turn away. I wouldn't have asked if I didn't want to hear." He lifted her hand, placing it inside his, running his thumb over her soft skin.

"Thank you. For some reason, I thought you would understand."

He hesitated before answering, then decided fuck it. He might as well offer her something in return for her honesty.

"I get it. I don't have a relative who suffers from depression but I ... I suffer from—" He stammered and wanted to take back the initial, tentative words that now stuck in his throat painfully. Though he'd thought he'd come to terms with this part of himself, embarrassment rushed through him now.

"I know." She squeezed his hand in hers, the silence understanding, not judgmental. "I *know*." She met his gaze, her expression warm and full of acceptance.

He didn't need to elaborate or use the word *anxiety*, because after only a short time in his employ, she did understand. She'd seen things firsthand. Walked in on him pulling out an anxiety medication. Remade his coffee when he couldn't drink it for reasons no one but him would understand. Put his clothes away in his closet exactly how he'd have done it himself.

Nothing he did or said had driven her away.

Before he could formulate a reply, the car came to a stop outside the venue in the financial district downtown. Formerly the headquarters of a major bank, the facility was now a landmark building in the National Historic Register, and a lineup of black Town Cars and drivers surrounded them.

"We can talk later," he said, although he selfishly hoped there'd be less talking and more *other things* before the night was through.

"Thank you." She leaned close, treating him to an up-close-and-personal whiff of her scent, one that was new to her but with a hint of the sweetness he always associated with this woman.

And as she pressed her lips to his cheek, his cock, which he'd managed to contain, now pressed hard and insistently against his pants. Thank God his jacket would cover the tenting or he wouldn't be able to get out of the car.

She pulled back, then giggled, the sound light and airy and perfect to break the serious moment and put them in a better mood for the night.

Reaching over, she rubbed her fingers against his cheek. "Lipstick," she murmured.

"Cover me in it any time," he said in return.

Her sexy lips parted in an O just as the driver opened the door, breaking into their moment.

Kade stepped out of the car, holding Lexie's hand as she did the same. He'd never thought about how he looked arriving at an event, but with Lexie on his arm, he was damned proud to be there.

"Those ships, they're gorgeous," Lexie said of a large 225-foot mural covering the back wall.

"It's spectacular," he agreed, hoping she wouldn't ask who painted it.

Kade didn't bother himself with art, so he couldn't name the creator. He only knew, from previous years at this event, the mural was always a talking piece, and clearly Lexie agreed.

No sooner had they stepped into the ballroom than people came up to Kade. The co-chairs of the event, to thank him for his substantial donation, potential investors in Blink, all people he needed to be more than polite to—when all he wanted to do was find a private corner and be alone with Lexie. He glanced her way often, worried about ignoring or, worse, boring her. But each time he looked, she was interested in the discussion he was having, talking to someone's wife while the men talked business, or waiting patiently for the person to have their say.

She didn't whine or complain, for which he was grateful, but she also genuinely seemed to enjoy herself, and that had been his goal for the evening. Not his only goal, he thought, using a rare moment alone to look his fill of the siren in the black-and-white dress. He couldn't take his eyes off the whole package, but he particularly liked the shorter hem in the front that teased him with the idea of lifting the dress higher and slipping his hands up her thighs and over her damp sex.

"Wine or champagne?" a passing server asked, breaking into his thoughts just in the nick of time.

"Thank you." Lexie accepted a glass of champagne.

Kade picked up a flute for himself and turned to face her.

"Excuse me." A man with a camera around his neck, obviously the hired photographer for the event, interrupted them. "May I?"

Resigned and aware this picture would show up somewhere in the papers or online tomorrow, Kade stepped closer to Lexie and wrapped his injured hand around her back. The photographer snapped a quick shot and disappeared, on to the next couple.

"Now where was I?" he asked, then held up his glass. "To … new beginnings."

She hesitated before tilting her glass, touching his.

If he weren't so sure the chemistry between them was hot and mutual, he'd be concerned with her reticence. But she was here, and when he wasn't looking directly at her, she was sneaking glimpses of him. Whatever had her uncertain, it wasn't a lack of attraction or desire.

"I like it when we're not bickering," she mused.

"Is that what we do? I thought it was you calling me out on asshole behavior."

She grinned and took a sip, allowing the bubbles to slide down her throat. He couldn't look away, his gaze drawn to the slender column of her neck, his hearing attuned to the purr of approval that escaped her lips. "Mmm."

"If you make that sound again, I just might drag you into the nearest coat closet and fuck you sense-less."

She choked on a sip of champagne, and heat

tinged her cheeks, her mouth parting in a silent O. Add in the sudden hitch in her breathing and he knew she was as into the idea as he was.

Not that he'd take her that way their first time, but he couldn't deny the notion had distinct appeal. He reined in his inappropriate thoughts because his dick was standing at attention and they were in a ballroom full of people. Nothing had been discussed about taking whatever their relationship was to that next level. But he wanted to.

He placed his glass on the table just as a familiar voice called out his name. "Kade!"

He turned. "Dad!" he exclaimed, taken off guard.

"Dad?" Lexie asked, surprise etching her features.

Shit. He'd forgotten his father was also a major donor at this event because it was important to Kade. Say what you want about his father, but he tried to please his son any way he could.

"Don't look so shocked to see me. I'm here every year, just like you," his dad said.

But Kade had been so wrapped up in thinking about Lexie and in the issues with Julian, he'd forgotten. "It's good to see you, Dad."

His father pulled him into a bear hug, and Kade returned the gesture, aware of Lexie's eyes on him the entire time.

"What did you do to your hand?" his father asked,

concerned, as he glanced at the splint.

"Nothing. Just an accident."

He frowned before meeting Kade's gaze once more. "Well, it's been too long. You really need to come visit your father." Keith turned to Lexie, a wide smile on his face. "And who is the pretty young lady?" he asked before Kade could get a word in to introduce her.

"Lexie Parker," she said, extending her hand. "I'm Kade's a—"

"Date. She's my date," he said before she could put the *assistant* barrier between them. Which he was certain she'd been about to do, and he wanted to know *why*.

But he also jumped in and clarified things, more for her benefit than his father's. Because his goal at the end of the night was to convince her to come home with him after the event ended. Anything less was unacceptable, and if she started thinking about the fact that she worked for him, he wouldn't be able to get her into his bed.

His father's smile widened at the pronouncement that Lexie was his date. "It's great to meet you, Lexie. Kade doesn't normally bring a date to these events, so it's a real treat."

"Dad," Kade said in warning. He didn't need the old man embarrassing him with details about his life.

But Keith was on a roll and continued, ignoring Kade's irate tone. "It's even rarer that I get to meet someone he's seeing so—"

"Dad! Can you give it a rest? Please?" Kade asked, annoyed he didn't just drop it.

Keith waved a hand in a dismissive gesture. "Oh, please. Let a father be happy for his son. She's a beautiful woman."

"Yes, she certainly is," Kade agreed.

Lexie blushed a deep crimson. "Thank you," she murmured.

"So, Lexie Parker, tell me about yourself." His father focused on her and waited for a reply.

Which didn't come. Lexie squirmed, obviously uncomfortable beneath his father's assessing gaze.

"Lexie works at Blink," Kade said, taking over in the wake of her silence. "She keeps everything around me running smoothly," he went on. "I couldn't function without her."

"He exaggerates," she said softly, so un-Lexie-like. She usually spoke her mind.

Keith looked from Lexie to Kade and grinned. "Well, I'll be damned. You found a woman to put up with your—"

"Isn't that Colton James?" Kade gestured to the far side of the room, where his father's oldest friend in the investment world stood with his wife. He interrupted before his father could discuss Kade's issues out loud and in public.

They might be at a benefit for mental illness, but Kade's quirks and anxieties were his own. He didn't like or choose to share himself with the world, and he wasn't about to start now.

His father looked across the room and nodded. "I need to have a word with Colton, actually. I'll catch up with you two later. Have fun," he said with a wink before heading for the opposite corner from where they were standing.

Lexie blew out a long, relieved breath, and Kade knew exactly how she was feeling. The air was lighter with his father gone.

But now that they were alone, his mind immediately returned to earlier, when she'd avoided admitting she was his date. "Why did you do that?" he asked her.

"Do what?" She took a sip of her now warm champagne, grimaced, and placed it on the nearest table.

"Why didn't you want to admit you're my date?" he asked. "Are you embarrassed to be with me?"

The words came out without prior thought or warning. After all, his father had alluded to him finding someone to put up with him, and the women in his past hadn't been able to.

"God, Kade, no!" Lexie sounded horrified at the

thought. "It's the opposite, actually. I was afraid your father would think I wasn't good enough for you!"

He reared back in shock. "Why the hell would you think that?"

Her face turned pale at his gruff tone, her blue eyes lighter against her fair skin. "I... It's just... You're *you*. You're intelligent, brilliant, really. And I'm ... me. I'm not sure if you ever looked at my resume, but I haven't held a long-term, stable job. And I lost my last one because I was chronically late due to ... family issues. And I was only hired because Derek took pity on me, and now I pick up your dry cleaning and order your lunches."

Kade hadn't thought beyond his own issues. He'd never had an inkling that his in-your-face assistant, the Lexie he admired, had her own insecurities she hid from the world.

He shook his head and groaned. "Aren't we a pair?" he asked ruefully.

"Are we?" she asked, her eyes bright, alight with renewed fire and interest.

"Fuck it," he muttered. "Let's get out of here." He grabbed her hand with his splint-free one and pulled her out of the gala, ignoring the stares of people as they passed.

"Kade!" He came to a halt at the sound of her voice, then pulled her into an alcove where they could be relatively alone.

"What's the rush?" she asked.

"I have the sudden urge to kiss you." Well, to do more than that, but even he knew he needed to finesse her more than he'd done so far.

Heat flared in her eyes. "So do it."

As if to back up her words, she rose onto her tiptoes and raised her chin. He met her halfway, pulling her flush against him and covering her mouth with his. She moaned and wrapped her arms around his neck, deepening their connection.

So much for worrying about finesse, he thought, losing himself in her sweetness and desire. A desire so hot it matched his.

His height had her tipping her neck, and he lifted her in his arms, grateful for the weight lifting he did at the gym because he had just one hand to work with. She came willingly, practically climbing him to get closer. He lived and breathed her in the space of this one kiss. Their tongues dueled, mouths devoured, and his body tightened with an all-consuming need.

Noise sounded from down the hall, and awareness of where they were returned to him. He forced himself to break the kiss, touching his forehead to hers. She inhaled deeply, catching her breath, while he did the same.

Finally, she eased back, meeting his gaze.

Her lips were moist and puffy, her eyes glazed with desire. "Kade?"

"Yes?" he asked, still searching for a calm he didn't feel, along with a way to walk out of that hallway without anyone noticing the hard-on that wouldn't be going away any time soon.

A smile meant just for him curved her lips. "Take me home," she whispered in a husky voice that wouldn't be denied.

LEXIE WAS BOLD in her everyday life. She could face off with anyone and hold her own—she'd all but dared Kade to kiss her, after all. And he clearly desired her, as evidenced not just by the way he'd dragged her out of the room but by the hot kiss they'd just shared and the hard ridge of his cock pressed insistently against her core. Even so, it had taken every ounce of courage she possessed to tell Kade she wanted to go home. With him.

One look into his darkened green eyes and her worry disappeared. He was definitely a man on the edge, in agreement with exactly what she wanted. And she had no doubt she wanted him. She'd never felt closer to a man, and she didn't mean physically, though she was still wrapped around him like a vine on a tree.

He'd opened up to her in the limo, admitting he suffered from certain … *disorders*. He didn't need to elaborate. She already understood him so well. But the fact that he'd try to ease her pain over her mother's illness by stripping himself bare emotionally touched something inside her. She'd told herself she couldn't have a relationship, and that still might be true, but she didn't want to walk away from him now.

Didn't she deserve to grab something for herself? Hadn't she given enough of her life and her time to her sister and mother? Without a doubt, she knew the time would come when her twin disrupted her life yet again, but tonight, while it was quiet and peaceful, she was taking what she wanted.

And she wanted Kade.

No sooner were they back in the limo than Kade pushed a button, and a divider slid up. Between the privacy divider and the tinted windows, they were cocooning in their own world.

Kade pushed another button and spoke to the driver. "Drive around until I tell you otherwise," he instructed.

His eyes were hot on hers, and a delicious shiver took hold, a premonition of what was to come. The scent of his musky cologne surrounded her, and it was all she could do not to crawl into his lap and make herself at home.

"Lie back," he said in a deep, seductive voice.

Trembling, she eased back against the far door, and he lifted her legs over his thighs, sliding across the seat until her ass was almost in his lap. Excitement licked through her as his big hand cupped her exposed calf ... and worked its way up her leg, his thumb caressing her skin in a slow, deliberate glide.

Arousal, warm and wet, trickled onto her upper leg, and her pussy clenched with desire and need. His finger reached the crease at her thigh, and he traced a line, closer and closer to her aching sex, reaching beneath her panties.

"I can make you feel good," he said in a thick voice, his teasing finger sliding in a barely there swipe over her clit.

Her hips bucked upward, but he didn't immediately offer her relief.

"What do you want? I need to hear you say it," he said.

"More," she whispered.

He pulled down her underwear, then slicked his finger over the outer lips of her sex in a deliberate tease. He added a second finger as he touched her everywhere but where she needed friction the most.

"Kade, please."

"Please what?" he asked, a determined glint in his eyes. "The words, Lexie, and I'll give you everything you want and need."

Who knew he had such a sadistic streak? she thought, the gnawing emptiness growing with every second he waited, torturing her with delayed gratification. His fingers continued to taunt her with deliberate strokes, back and forth, over and over, until her hips rose in time to his ministrations.

"Touch me," she begged, her voice catching.

"Where?" he asked through a clenched jaw.

She didn't do dirty talk, but if that's what it would take for him to give her relief, she'd do it.

"And look at me when you ask."

He wisped his finger over her clit, not hard enough to satisfy, just enough to leave her emptier than before.

She met and held his gaze. "Touch my sex."

"More."

She was near to weeping now. "Touch my pussy. My clit. Make me come, Kade, please." She begged and waited breathlessly for his touch.

He shoved her dress higher and pulled her panties partway down her legs. "We missed dinner," he said before lowering his head and swiping at her clit with his warm, wet tongue. "And I'm starved."

She moaned loudly, and he began devouring her in earnest. He lapped at her juices and took her out of her head, to a place where pleasure reigned and all she could focus on was the feel of his mouth against her sex. She ground her hips against him, the pleasure intense and growing, rising, quickly becoming an inferno ready to explode.

She reached down. Grabbed his hair. Pressed him harder against her sex, and suddenly her orgasm struck, her entire body swept under by its power. Waves pummeled her from all sides, inside and out, her hoarse cries echoing in the back of the enclosed car.

He gentled his touch, taking her down slowly, still licking her, this time gently, until she collapsed, spent, against the uncomfortable door.

He wiped his mouth against her thigh, then pressed a soft kiss to her skin before raising his head and meeting her gaze.

"Delicious," he said, pulling her panties back up her legs.

Barely able to process what had just occurred, she watched in silence as he righted her dress, smoothing the front down over her legs.

"Good?" he asked.

Her lips parted, but no words came out, so she nodded.

He leaned over, pressing the button he'd touched before. "We can go home now," he said to the driver.

"Very good, sir."

Her mouth was dry, and she licked her lips, forcing herself to meet his gaze. Did she say thank you? Or *it's your turn later*?

Before she could decide, he spoke her name. "Lexie?"

"Yes?"

"In case you were wondering, it's soundproof back here."

Her cheeks flamed as the car sped toward his apartment building, where she was certain more pleasure—hers and his—was waiting.

Chapter Nine

K ADE USED THE time during the ride back to his place to get his breathing—and his cock—under control. He knew Lexie was sweet. He just hadn't known how much he'd enjoy giving her pleasure and not worrying about his own. He'd needed to hear what she desired. He hadn't wanted her frustrated, but he did need her begging for something only he could give. She hadn't disappointed him.

He hoped she never would.

He kept an arm around her after they left the car and made their way to his apartment. Inside, they each kicked off their shoes. Once they were comfortable, he offered her food because, as he'd pointed out, they'd skipped dinner.

She declined. Instead, she pushed him back against the wall and began fumbling with his pants, her need apparently not sated by what he hoped was just the first of many orgasms tonight.

She pushed his slacks down his hips, taking his boxer briefs along with them. He kicked them aside. She gripped his cock in her small hand, gliding her hand down his shaft, tightening at the base before she slid up again, only to swipe at the pre-come pooling at the tip.

He saw stars behind his eyes, need pounding at him, his balls tight against his body.

"Condoms are in the bedroom," he told her.

In reply, she sank to her knees.

Holy fuck.

That, he hadn't expected.

She didn't hesitate either. She slid her mouth over his cock, slowly but surely, enclosing him in wet heat. One hand gripping him, she began to suck, pulling him deep and easing off, teasing him with her tongue and sliding back and forth along his shaft.

His hands came to her head, and he began to pump his hips, taking care not to push too hard too fast. He didn't need to worry. She picked up a perfect rhythm on her own, working his cock, doing exactly what he liked, reading him as if they'd been together for a while.

His balls ached, and he was seconds away from coming, so he pulled back, easing out of her eager mouth. "No fucking way am I coming this first time without being buried in your pussy."

Her eyes glazed over, and she nodded in eager agreement. He placed an arm beneath her elbow and helped her up. Grasping her hand, he pulled her to the bedroom, where his large king-size bed waited.

As if choreographed, she turned, and he knew to unzip her dress, exposing the long lines of her back before letting the garment fall to the floor. He traced a finger down her spine and she shivered. He then pulled her underwear down, kneeling so she could step out of them.

He couldn't resist cupping one soft globe of her ass in his hand, squeezing tight. She moaned, turning toward him, bringing him face-to-face with her luscious rounded breasts and darkened nipples, already tight with desire. A glance lower and he saw her neatly trimmed pussy, glistening with need.

"Beautiful," he said, referring to the whole package, as he undid the cuffs on his shirt.

Her cheeks flushed but she didn't duck in embarrassment. She merely reached out and began unbuttoning his shirt, unfastening each one until she slid the garment to the floor.

He stripped off the rest of his clothes. "Come on," he said gruffly, pulling her onto the bed along with him.

He paused to pull a condom from the nightstand

and roll it onto his aching member. Then, knowing he couldn't brace both hands on the mattress with his bad hand, he rolled onto his back and pulled her on top of him. She braced her legs on either side of his hips and settled herself above his straining cock.

"I've wanted this since I first laid eyes on you," he admitted, surprising himself.

An appreciative smile lifted her lips. "Same here." She met his gaze, her eyes a smoky blue as she slowly lowered herself onto his thick, straining erection.

"Come on, you can take me."

She let out a husky laugh. "Umm ... you're bigger than I imagined." She blushed and settled herself onto him completely, taking him to a heaven he'd never thought existed.

Her inner walls cushioned him tight in moist heat, a perfect fit. Before he could think, she started to move, gliding up and down on his shaft. He couldn't breathe, could only get lost in the perfection he found inside her body.

Needing to touch her, he grasped her hip with one hand, holding on as she rode him, her hot sheath clasping around him. Up and down, grinding as their bodies collided, meshing together, melding. Heat flooded him, and his heart pumped hard inside his chest, his body close to soaring.

"Not coming without you," he said, holding back

despite the blood boiling in his veins.

Her cheeks were flushed, her lips parted, sweet satisfaction on her face.

He glanced down, his gaze taking in his cock, slick with her arousal, being swallowed up by her body.

"Again," he muttered, entranced by the sight.

She bit down on her lower lip and pushed herself up, revealing his long length before she dropped down on him once more. "Oh God, I'm close."

Her words took him by surprise, inflaming his need even more. "Then come," he ordered.

At his command, she clenched her thighs tighter and pitched forward, her pubic bone hitting his. She cried out, the beginning of her orgasm crashing over her, and she rocked harder, grasping his wrist, holding on as she rode out the waves. He watched her, a vision as her breasts bounced and her body trembled, all for him.

"Kade!" His name on her lips triggered his release, and he came harder than ever, his entire body overcome by swells of ecstasy the likes of which he'd never known.

LEXIE SAT IN bed with Kade, eating freshly delivered pizza right out of the box. For a man who liked his desk immaculate and his closet hangers just so, she was surprised he didn't mind the crumbs in his bed. She was equally surprised by how at ease she felt with him *after*. He'd helped her off him, accompanied her to the bathroom to clean up, where they'd ended up sharing a fast shower, quick only because their stomachs were growling from the lack of sustenance all evening.

He'd lent her a tee shirt, declined her offer to leave, which she had to admit set her heart fluttering again. As if the amazing orgasms he'd given her in the car and in his bed, weren't enough to have her smiling wide.

"I love cheesy pizza," she said, placing the crust down and wiping her fingers on a napkin. The garlicky scent smelled like heaven to her.

"Me too." He grabbed a napkin of his own.

She glanced over. His hair was a mess, but he was the sexiest thing she'd ever laid eyes on. "You know, I'm surprised you don't mind ... the mess." She gestured to the box and balled up napkins.

He stilled.

"I'm sorry. I didn't mean—"

"No. I need to explain." He threw all the garbage into the box and placed the cardboard onto the floor before turning back to her. "Where do I begin?"

She curled her legs beneath her and clasped his hand in hers. "Wherever you're comfortable. I'm listening."

He ducked his head, not meeting her gaze as he began to speak. "I wasn't the easiest child, and I mean that seriously as well as literally."

"Geniuses rarely are," she said, hoping to lighten the moment.

His mouth lifted, and she caught sight of the dimple she thought was so hot.

"The thing is, my mother didn't think I was smart. She didn't think I was anything but an annoyance she didn't want to deal with."

She gasped, unable to hold back her horrified reaction.

A muscle worked in his jaw as he spoke, and suddenly she hated a woman she'd never even met.

"It's okay. I've accepted it." His laugh was harsh. "Anyway, you saw the picture of my brother, right?"

"Yeah." She held her breath, grateful for the information he'd chosen to share.

"Jeffrey. He's younger than me, and he was so much easier. Your golden child."

"There's no such thing," she said softly, still holding his hand in hers.

"Tell that to her." His body jerked inadvertently. "Apparently I came into the world with colic, and it went downhill from there." He breathed more heavily now, the admission obviously painful. "I had problems in school, difficulties making friends, trouble concentrating, and then there's anxiety. None of which was diagnosed back then. So she constantly told me I was a pain in the ass, that she wished I was more like my brother, and in the end, she chose Jeffrey."

Lexie narrowed her gaze. "How so?"

"My parents divorced … and my loving mother took my brother and moved to England, never to be heard from again."

"Oh, Kade." No wonder he'd reacted so strongly when he'd found her with the photo.

"You know the strange thing? I never resented Jeffrey. Not once. I looked up to him."

"I'm sure he felt the same way about you."

Kade shrugged. "I'll never know."

"Have you ever reached out?" she asked.

"No. I wasn't about to set myself up for rejection."

More rejection, she thought, grasping his hand harder. She swallowed hard, unsure of what to say.

"But back to what you asked me, about the pizza and the mess?"

She waved away the question. It no longer mattered, in light of everything else.

"The answer is, I don't know. I can't control what my brain chooses to obsess over. And the medicine I take helps a lot. So did the CBT sessions."

"CBT?"

"Cognitive behavioral therapy. It helps solve problems and change thinking patterns." He shrugged, jerking out of her grasp, obviously embarrassed.

"Don't pull away from me."

"You should go." He rose from the bed. He wore only a pair of track pants, and his bare chest heaved heavily as he breathed. "You will eventually. Might as well—"

"No." Instead of being insulted, she understood. Enough people had left her for her to recognize the same fear in him.

She climbed out of bed. Coming up beside him, she placed a hand on his shoulder, the muscles hard and tense beneath her palm.

"Don't assume I'm like everyone else you know or might have been with, because that's just insulting." This was no time to get into her history or her past. All he needed to know now was that she wouldn't run away just because he didn't fit some cookie-cutter mold. "You can't scare me off," she informed him.

He spun back around. "No?" he asked, admiration in his tone, appreciation in his gaze.

"No." She rocked back on her heels so she could look up and better meet his gaze.

He shook his head and smiled, all the tension leaving his body in a rush of air. "You, Lexie Parker, are something else."

She grinned, pleased she'd broken through his barriers and gotten through to him. "Yeah?" she asked.

"Yeah. The question is, what am I going to do with you?"

"I can think of a few things." She waggled her eyebrows before lifting the hem of his shirt and pulling it over her head.

And those were the last words spoken for a good, long while.

KADE WOKE UP to the sun streaming through his window and a warm, soft body beside him in bed.

Lexie.

He didn't typically have women over. Sex? Yes. At their place, not his. He didn't like his privacy invaded, and he loathed the awkward mornings after. Something he hadn't given a thought when he'd taken Lexie home with him or when they had finally passed out from exhaustion last night. Or should he say from exertion?

He couldn't remember the last time he'd felt so relaxed or complete. He didn't want to get ahead of himself or assume too much. Nor did he want to overthink the way he'd spilled his guts last night. It wasn't his finest moment, yet she hadn't flinched, except to be outraged on his behalf, which he had to admit had made him feel good.

So he decided to begin the day the same way they'd ended last night. He rolled her onto her back and tossed the covers aside. Starting at her jaw, he kissed her, working his way down her body. He licked at her jaw, slid his tongue down her neck, and nipped at her collarbone.

She moaned, obviously awake. "Good morning," he said, lapping at the soft skin of first one breast, then the other.

"Good morn—Aah!" Her words turned to a moan when he latched his mouth around her nipple and began to tease her with his tongue and teeth. She grasped his head, keeping him tight against her chest while she writhed and moaned beneath him.

His cock pressed hard against her thigh, aching and painful, needing release. But he wasn't focused on himself.

"Kade," she murmured.

"Hmm?"

"I want to taste you too," she said, reaching for his dick.

He raised himself up on one arm. "Yeah?"

"Yeah," she said, eyes glazed with desire.

He shifted positions so his head was level with her sweet pussy and his cock was near her mouth. He swiped his tongue across her clit, and she arched into him, but she also gripped his shaft in one hand and licked the head, coating him in moist heat.

"Fuck." It was his turn to groan.

She pulled him into her mouth, and stars flickered behind his eyes. It was all he could do not to thrust deep and hit the back of her throat, to keep pumping until he came. But he managed to hold back and instead retain his focus on her, sliding his tongue over her sex and nipping at her with his teeth.

She bucked, her hips thrusting forward. He grasped her thigh, holding on as he devoured her, doing his damnedest to deal with the heat and rising tide of desire flooding his body while making sure she came first.

He nudged his nose into her sex, her scent intoxicating, her taste delicious. Addicting. She pumped his shaft, her hand tight around the base, his balls drawing up tight.

Without warning, she stilled, then began to tremble, shake, and moan around his cock. The vibrations set off his own orgasm, and before he could warn her, he came hard and fast, waves of unbelievable pleasure washing over him, pulling him further under her spell.

THE TWO WEEKS after the gala were like living a dream. Their photograph showed up on Page Six of the *New York Post*, online and in print, something Lexie wasn't used to at all. She actually clipped the picture as a memento of a special night they'd shared and tucked it away in her dresser drawer.

Most women had many experiences with the highs and honeymoon period of dating a new guy, and all the fun and euphoria that entailed. Not Lexie. John was her last serious boyfriend. She'd known then and there, if he couldn't put up with the drama in her family, no one could. Kade had swept in and just taken over, and for now, with her sister occupied with a new guy whom Lexie had yet to meet, she could enjoy their time together. Still, knowing her sister was on a high, even with new meds, Lexie waited for the next fall. Even with the real fear in the background, she felt like she was living a dream, and she didn't want to wake up.

Her job stayed the same. She would arrive before Kade and wait to bring him his coffee, but with the shift in their relationship, he seemed to find more ways for her to help him out—and spend more time with her during the day. At night, they went out for dinner after work and often ended up at his apartment for a Mario Party match or other video game he patiently taught her.

One night, his father surprised him by showing up and inviting them to dinner. Kade hadn't appreciated the interruption, but she'd convinced him to go, and he'd wanted her with him. That he'd want her around his family made her feel warm and fuzzy inside.

More than once, she'd battled with herself over how much to tell him about her sister. It wasn't that she was embarrassed. After all, she'd already admitted the painful truth about her mother. It's just that she knew in her heart that Kendall would eventually force Lexie to choose between helping her or being there for Kade. Bringing Kendall into her relationship with him could happen later. For now she wanted to live in her happy bubble a little while longer.

Even if that bubble still included picking up his dry cleaning, dropping it at the store, and delivering the clean clothes back to his apartment every Tuesday and Saturday.

She had lunch plans with her sister this particular Saturday, because Kendall had been busy with Jay and Lexie had spent many late nights with Kade. They hadn't really talked in a while.

"Kendall, let's go! If we're going to make our lunch reservation, we need to get this dry cleaning run finished!" Lexie called from the kitchen.

"Coming!" Kendall came out of her bedroom, a broad smile on her face … wearing an outfit Lexie had never seen before. A pair of tight jeans, a style Kendall had never chosen before, a purple top, and a white leather jacket. "Ready!" her sister said, joining her in the family room.

Lexie liked seeing her sister in a good mood and bit her tongue on the new clothes. She already knew there'd been shopping bags in her sister's room, and Kendall had blown off the conversation when Lexie mentioned it earlier in the week. She wasn't going to get anywhere now, and it would only ruin their day.

"Okay, let's head out," Lexie said, grabbing her handbag and slinging it over her shoulder.

"I can't believe you pick up your boyfriend's dry cleaning, drop it off, and head back to his place again with his clean clothes." She wrinkled her nose in disgust.

"I prefer to think of this as just doing my job. Kade isn't home. He's at a business meeting with an investor who's in from out of town."

"Oh, I get to see where your boyfriend lives!" Kendall said, sounding excited by the prospect.

Lexie grabbed her keys from the entryway credenza as they passed. "You can see the building from the taxi. You're not coming inside."

Kendall frowned. "Party pooper."

Ignoring her, Lexie followed her sister into the hall. A little while later, they'd stopped at Kade's to pick up his dirty laundry. As she'd requested, Kendall waited in the cab, bitching about being left behind.

They headed to the cleaner's, where Lexie handed in his clothing, giving specific instructions about his shirts and pressed pants, despite the fact that the same store cleaned his clothing every week. He required the instructions be said out loud each time, so she followed his directions exactly.

Finally, they returned to his apartment, Kade's cleaning spread out on Lexie's lap. She climbed out of the cab. "Be right back. Please wait again," Lexie said.

She'd warned the driver ahead of time there would be a lot of errands and waiting. Kade didn't mind the bill. Lexie climbed out of the car, lifting the cleaning higher so it didn't drag on the ground.

As she approached the doorman, her sister ran up beside her. "Get back in the car," Lexie said, annoyed.

"Oh, come on. I just want to see where your rich boyfriend lives," Kendall said, too loud for Lexie's liking.

She turned to face her twin. "There's no reason for you to come up with me. I'll be right back."

Kendall pursed her lips in a pout. "Come on, please? Time's wasting and the meter's running. Let's just go. Please?"

Lexie groaned. "Fine. Just stick close," she muttered, glad Kade wasn't home. The first time she introduced him to her sister, Lexie wanted time to prepare herself for any eventuality.

Lexie disarmed the alarm and let them inside.

"Oh, wow," Kendall said, her mouth opening wide as she took in the large apartment. "Talk about a big screen!" she said, heading straight for the den area. "I love this cinema-like sofa!" Without asking, she threw herself into one of the seats and hit the electronic button that moved her seat back.

"Kendall, get up!" Lexie said, beyond annoyed. "You're wearing dark jeans. New dark jeans. They could rub off on the white leather. Don't go near anything else."

The electronic whir of the seat followed. "Man, you're uptight. Is he that much of a stick in the mud?" Kendall asked.

"No. You just weren't invited here." Lexie shot her sister a glare. "I'll get the clothes put away, and we can be on our way."

Lexie took the clothes into the bedroom and stepped into Kade's walk-in closet. She pulled the plastic off his shirts and hung them up, taking care to leave the same amount of space between each and to line them up by color. She did the same with his slacks. There weren't too many because he was a casual guy and Helen did his everyday laundry. Still, he'd had meetings, so he'd used his dress clothes a few times this week.

"This bedroom is gorgeous!" Kendall's voice carried. "I bet this bed is ultra-comfortable too."

"Just don't test it out," she called back of the extremely cozy bed that was nice and large, with ample room for her to spread out and part her legs so Kade could fit his broad body in between when he licked her pussy and brought her to the most explosive orgasms.

She shivered at the reminder, her nipples perking up. *Nope, not this afternoon,* she thought. No sex until tonight. She grinned and gathered the plastic to throw it in the garbage before she left.

She found her twin waiting in the hallway near the front door. Apparently Lexie's chiding had accomplished something, and Kendall had behaved better while she did her job. She tossed the garbage in the pail hidden behind a wood door in the kitchen.

"Ready for lunch?" Lexie said.

"Actually I'm not feeling well. I have a headache," Kendall said, shifting from foot to foot, suddenly antsy.

"I'm sorry. But I'm sure food will help your head. We'll just go get lunch and—"

"No. I want to go home and lie down," Kendall insisted, grabbing Lexie's arm and leading her toward the elevator. "I don't want it to turn into a migraine."

Lexie glanced at her sister, concerned by her sudden change in behavior.

"If your head hurts that badly, of course we'll go home." Even if she wasn't convinced that Kendall had a headache after all.

Chapter Ten

KADE HEADED FOR lunch at an exclusive Italian restaurant in Midtown Manhattan with one of Blink's key investors, Ian Dare. Normally Kade would enjoy meeting up with Ian, an old college buddy, but Ian had made it clear today's meeting was about business. Ian had flown in from Miami on his private jet, specifically to discuss something about Blink going public and Ian's financial contribution to the IPO, the Initial Public Offering.

Kade's stomach clenched, and acid burned in his gut, but he pasted a big smile on his face and joined Ian, who was already waiting at a table in the back of the small restaurant. As usual, Ian wore a suit, and expecting that, Kade had dressed up himself, choosing a pair of black slacks and a white button-down shirt.

"Ian, good to see you," Kade said, shaking hands with his old friend.

"Same." Ian pumped his hand and the two men sat down.

"Derek and Luke send their best." Kade shook his napkin out in front of him.

"Get into a fight?" Ian asked, gesturing to Kade's injury and the splint covering his fingers and knuckles.

Kade didn't see the point in lying. "I took my frustration out on a wall. The wall won." He smirked at himself, because what else could he do?

Ian laughed. "I've wanted to do that a few times myself."

"How's your beautiful wife and daughter?" Kade asked, changing the subject to one that always put Ian in a good mood.

He grinned, leaning back in his chair. "Fantastic. Riley's pregnant again," Ian said.

If Kade wasn't mistaken, the other man was fucking beaming. "Congratulations. That calls for a drink." He gestured to the waiter.

Ian ordered himself a Glenlivet on the rocks.

Kade ordered his usual. "Macallan 18, neat, filled three quarters of the way full. I'll also take a fresh bottle of natural spring water, room temperature, and a straw please."

Ian raised an eyebrow but said nothing. It'd been years since Kade and Ian had shared a meal with drinks ordered, and the last time, they were college kids drinking beer.

"And your daughter?" Kade asked.

"Adorable, as you saw last time you were in town."

Kade laughed because Ian's little girl had indeed stolen the show at his mother's second wedding, as the flower girl.

The waiter returned a few minutes later with their drinks. He placed Kade's glass on the table, followed by a bottle of water and straw.

"May I?" the waiter asked.

Kade nodded.

The waiter poured water into a separate glass. Once the man left them alone, Kade took the straw and dipped it into the water, then placed exactly four drops into his scotch.

He raised his glass and spoke. "To your family," he said, wanting to express his honest feelings before they delved into more serious business matters. "To their health and happiness."

Ian clinked his glass. "Thanks, man."

Kade inclined his head.

The waiter started to walk over, and Kade waved him away.

"Let's talk first. That way we can enjoy the meal," he said to Ian, hoping that whatever his friend wanted was something Kade could address and put behind them.

Ian sobered, leaning in closer to keep their conversation private. "Listen, I know you're doing your damnedest to avoid a lawsuit with Julian that could derail Blink going public at a solid opening rate on the exchange."

Kade inclined his head, listening. Neither confirming nor denying. For now.

"You know I'm more than willing to ride it out. I trust the three of you. But the reason I asked to meet with you alone is that my people have heard rumblings about a threat to the deal going through. Something beyond Julian's claim on partnership."

Kade narrowed his gaze. "Like what?" Because he was in the thick of it, and he hadn't heard a damned thing … except the hidden landmine from his past.

But unless and until they completely shut Julian down, he wouldn't dare use the date rape accusation against him. That would be a sure way to guarantee he received nothing from his supposed involvement in Blink's infancy. He needed the leverage.

"Let's just say there's talk of something in your past coming back to bite you in the ass and derail the IPO. I don't know what, but it's enough to make me … and some of the institutional investors nervous."

Fuck. Kade shoved a hand through his hair before lowering his arm and letting his fingers run over the glass of his watch. He wasn't wearing the Patek, but the smoothness of the crystal beneath his fingers calmed him.

"Is there any truth to it?" Ian asked, then held up a hand before Kade could respond. "Let me rephrase. Is there anything for me to worry about?"

"No," Kade immediately promised his friend. "Your money is safe. The company is fine. The IPO will go forward."

Whatever was going on with that bastard Julian, Kade had no doubt he was behind the rumors, trying to rattle Kade and push him into over-settling. That wouldn't happen. Kade would admit the truth himself and step aside before he'd let a company he'd worked his ass off creating be derailed. Nor would he let his friends lose out on gains they deserved.

"Fair enough." Ian, always a man of few words, didn't ask for more.

Kade understood Ian had flown all the way in to look him in the eye and get reassurance. Knowing the lengths he'd go to in order to protect Derek, Luke, and Blink, Kade had no problem giving it to him.

"Then let's order food."

For the next hour, Kade and Ian talked about the football team Ian was president of, the Miami Thunder, and their chances for another Super Bowl run. Ian filled him in on his family, and Kade talked about the excitement of taking Blink public.

They were waiting for the check when Ian asked, "So, anyone serious in your life?"

Good thing Kade had finished his drink, because he hadn't been prepared for the question and would definitely have choked on his scotch.

"I'm seeing someone," he said vaguely. Since the gala, Lexie had become increasingly entrenched in his life.

Not only because she was his PA and they spent even more time together, at work and outside of it, but because he couldn't stop thinking of her. She filled his waking and non-waking thoughts in a way no woman ever had. None. Because she understood him on a level no one had bothered to reach before her.

He liked to think he got her the same way. On the outside, she was tough, capable of standing up to him at his most difficult and able to cope with a less-than-easy family life. The pain her mother's illness caused her was never far from her mind. He often saw her eyes glaze, and she would go somewhere distant and painful. Kade knew how much it hurt to lose someone close to you. True, his mother had left by choice, but Lexie's mother was gone just the same. And that was a hurt he could comprehend deeply.

Ian grinned. "That's good. I want you to find what I did with Riley," he said, breaking into Kade's thoughts.

"Don't rush it. We're just beginning." Kade wanted to believe they filled an empty space in each other's lives, but any time he let himself have faith, fear returned, lodging in the pit of his stomach.

Ian studied him intently. "The idea of one woman for the rest of your life used to spook you. Don't waste time on nerves or worrying about things you can't control." The man always had a way of seeing deeply and getting to the heart of the matter. "I did that, and I nearly lost the most important thing in my life."

Kade didn't know Ian and Riley's history, but before her, no one woman had been able to pin Ian down. "How'd you do it?" Kade asked.

"Do what?"

"Stop … worrying. Give up that control you mentioned." Because that's what scared Kade the most. Letting himself go into a freefall over a woman and having his heart ripped out of his chest. Although, he had to admit, he was pretty far gone for Lexie already.

"Who says I did?" Ian asked. "I said to stop worrying about things and just enjoy life. But when it comes to your woman, even if you don't have control, always, always maintain the illusion." Ian laughed, and Kade joined him because he'd seen Ian with Riley, and it was clear she had him wrapped around her finger. He just wouldn't be surprised if that changed inside the bedroom. A place Kade had no desire to go.

The waiter walked over, and Kade snagged the bill-fold before Ian could do the same, determined to treat his friend, considering he'd made the trip out of concern for his financial stake in Kade's company.

Ian scowled but let it go.

He left the lunch knowing he had to deal with the Julian situation sooner rather than later. But for the moment, he wanted to see Lexie.

LEXIE HAD EXPECTED an enjoyable lunch with her sister, but she'd forgotten the cardinal rule of living with Kendall. Never get too comfortable. No sooner had they left Kade's apartment than Kendall became agitated. She was unable to sit still, wouldn't look Lexie in the eye, and kept rubbing her hands on her thighs anxiously. She bailed on lunch, claiming she had a headache and wanted to go home and lie down. Lexie was skeptical but she'd agreed.

She also stayed close to home, her gut screaming that something bigger than a mere headache was going on, a hunch that was confirmed when Kendall bounced out of her room, grabbed her keys from the counter, and yelled, "Be back! Have to meet Jay."

Lexie blew out a long breath and settled on the

sofa with a book and Waffles by her side, to wait for her sister's return. She read and she dozed off. She wasn't sure how much time had passed, so she pulled out her phone, surprised to see it was late afternoon and she had a text from Kade.

Pleasure filled her at the sight of his name. She knew he had a lunch meeting with an old friend who was also a major investor in Blink. The timing worked perfectly because she'd had lunch with her sister, or she was supposed to.

Come by tonight?

Everything inside her wanted to see him. She wanted to lock the door and close them in alone, not just in his apartment but his bed. When she was alone with him, his big body covering hers, nothing existed but them.

With Kendall gone, there was nothing she could do to find out what was bothering her twin or help her at all. She lifted her fingers to respond to Kade with a big *YES, I'll see you soon*, when her sister barreled into the apartment, an anxiety-ridden mess.

"Hi," Lexie said, dropping her phone to the couch, putting her own wants on hold for the time being.

"Hi. Do we have any ice cream?" Kendall asked, opening the freezer and peering inside.

Lexie narrowed her gaze. "Where were you?"

"Out."

"I know that," Lexie said, her jaw clenched tightly. "You mentioned seeing Jay."

"Yeah. Oh! Mint chip. Yum." Kendall grabbed a spoon from the drawer, opened the container, and began to eat from the pint.

Lexie wrinkled her nose. "Can't you use a bowl?"

"No," she said, pacing as she ate.

Waffles, who had jumped off the couch when Kendall walked in, ran to her side. And as if sensing Kendall's distress, the dog began barking and dancing around Kendall's feet, as agitated as his owner.

"Is everything okay with Jay?" Lexie asked, pushing harder for answers.

"Yep. Why wouldn't it be?"

"Because one minute you were calm, happy, and we were set to go out for lunch. The next thing I knew, you canceled because you had a headache, but a few minutes later, you ran out of the apartment like it was on fire." Lexie pushed herself up from the sofa. "Kendall, what's wrong? I want to help."

"You're nagging me because I canceled lunch?" she asked in what was surely feigned disbelief. "How selfish can you be? I didn't feel well. Then Jay called and I was feeling better and I wanted to see him. Do you really have a problem with that?" Kendall rocked on her heels and looked everywhere but at Lexie.

She blew out a long, frustrated breath. "I have a

problem with you ruining my day too if you weren't really sick, but that's not the point. You're suddenly agitated and—"

"Oh! We're back to me being crazy?" Kendall asked, her voice rising. "I'm going to my room. Waffles, come!" She spun around and stormed toward her bedroom, leaving Lexie alone in the kitchen.

She grasped the counter, dizzy from her twin's mercurial mood swing. Especially since she'd been doing so well. A few weeks ago, this was behavior she'd have expected and was used to living with. Since she'd adjusted her meds, Kendall had seemed better, with fewer highs and lows. Today's had come out of nowhere.

God, she wanted nothing more than to escape by going over to Kade's, but if her sister truly was suddenly spiraling and she left her alone, there was a good chance she'd walk out of here later and head for a bar. Pick up a guy for quick, meaningless sex, despite having a boyfriend. Though it had been awhile since she'd exhibited such reckless behavior, Lexie wanted to be able to talk her out of it or join her and play buffer to her destructive tendencies.

She walked over to where she'd tossed her phone, a lump in her throat and pain in her chest. How many times in the past had she had to pass on something she wanted to do to play her sister's keeper? Too many to count, Lexie thought. But had she ever felt so bad before? Like she was suddenly on the verge of losing something she hadn't even known she desperately wanted? She swallowed hard, wanting to believe she was jumping to conclusions. She hadn't *lost* Kade. She was just skipping one night.

But that's how it started, a little voice reminded her. With guys, with friends, it always started innocently enough. A canceled plan here. A *sorry I can't make it* there. Until the guy or the friend stopped calling altogether.

She glanced at the closed bedroom door and flopped onto the couch in defeat. It didn't matter how Lexie felt. She was needed here, she thought, and picked up the phone to let Kade know she wouldn't be coming by tonight.

SORRY I CAN'T make it tonight. I'll see you at work on Monday.

Kade read Lexie's vague text with no explanation as to why, after spending most of their free time together, she suddenly just *couldn't make it.*

He settled in to eat meatloaf that Helen had prepared for him, wondering what she was doing tonight that was so important. More important than him. Not exactly the kind of thoughts he was used to having.

He frowned and rose from his seat, rinsing his plate off in the sink and placing it in the dishwasher.

His cell rang, and, figuring it was a good distraction from everything circling in his brain obsessively, he answered without checking who it was.

"Hello?"

"It's Evan Mann." The investigator Kade had left a message for after finishing lunch with Ian Dare. "Got your message, but I was tied up until now, and I have pictures you're going to want to see."

Kade raised an eyebrow. "What kind of pictures?"

"Your ex-partner and some chick. You and your partners said you wanted anything I could dig up. Well, this woman seems to be important to him. I sent them over to your email."

"Thanks. Does this woman have a name?" Kade asked, picking up his plate and carrying it to the sink.

"Working on that. More soon." Mann disconnected the call.

"Nice bedside manner," Kade muttered. He leaned against the counter and switched apps on his phone, opening his email.

Mann's message came through. Kade tapped the email, and a photograph loaded onto the screen.

A photo of Lexie and Julian.

He blinked, but the view on the screen stayed the same.

Lexie and Julian.

What. The. Fuck.

What was she doing with that bastard? Kade didn't want to believe she could betray him that way, but the proof was in his hands. He glanced down once more, taking in the delicate features he'd memorized, her small nose, full lips, and the hand he'd often held. That Julian was now holding.

Dammit!

He opened a cabinet and grabbed a scotch, taking a long swig straight from the bottle. Lexie. Sweet, caring, sexy Lexie. The woman he'd opened himself up to. The woman he'd showed his greatest weakness and to whom he'd revealed his flaws had played him.

He thought about texting her, but he wasn't about to put himself out there again, not even for an explanation there was no way he'd believe. He'd invited her tonight and she'd said no. Now he knew why.

End of story.

End of them.

His hands began to shake as reality set in. From their intimate position, it was clear they were close, physically and emotionally. She'd stabbed him in the back, and she wasn't the first female to do so.

He could make himself crazy, thinking about his long string of failures with women. He took another pull, letting the liquid burn down his throat. *His mother.*

Another mouthful of whiskey. *Angela*, the woman who'd stolen things from him and pawned them for cash. He chugged again. *Lila,* who'd accused him of date rape. He'd sworn never again, but his organized, gutsy assistant who'd held her own with him and played Mario Party like a champ had betrayed him.

He carried the bottle into his bedroom, and that was the last thing he remembered until the sun streamed through the window, waking him.

He rolled over and his head began to pound. His mouth felt like it was full of cotton. And the memory of the photograph on his phone flashed through his mind, an unwanted memory and a painful fact he didn't want to think about. Unfortunately, it was all he could do. Visualize Lexie and Julian.

Nausea rose, and somehow he managed not to lose all the alcohol he'd consumed last night. He reached for his watch on the nightstand and didn't find it. He sat up and, ignoring the throbbing in his head, looked at the empty place where he always kept his Patek Phillipe. The watch that soothed him. The same one he'd touched yesterday before he'd left the apartment to meet with Ian.

Before his entire life had gone to shit.

Where was it? Kade was ridiculously organized, and if there was one thing he wouldn't misplace, it was this particular timepiece.

He headed into the bathroom to brush his teeth, recounting yesterday in his head while he did so. He'd placed the watch on the nightstand and left to have lunch. Saturday was Helen's day off, but it was dry cleaning day, which meant ... Lexie had been to his apartment.

No, he thought, rinsing the toothbrush and replacing it in the holder. History would not fucking repeat itself. Lexie hadn't taken something that belonged to him. Not for any reason. But she'd been with Julian ... and he hadn't thought her capable of that either.

He returned to the bedroom and picked up the phone, dialing the doorman downstairs. "Joseph, this is Kaden Barnes. Penthouse. I was wondering if you could tell me who signed in yesterday?"

"Just Ms. Parker and she's on your approved list."

"Helen wasn't in?" But he felt guilty even asking. Helen had been with him for over two years, and she'd been an exemplary employee. She'd taken good care of him and had proven herself trustworthy.

"No sir."

"Thank you," Kade said, everything inside him withering even more.

How could he consistently choose wrong and pick women who stole from him and had no problem hurting him to get what they wanted? Did his money make him that much of an easy target? Or was he just that fucking stupid?

He raised his hand, but the splint on it mocked his ability to hit another wall.

His cell phone rang. Derek's name flashed on the screen. He hit accept. "Hey."

"Hey. Luke and I were going to get brunch at that fancy new place that makes killer mimosas. The one near the office. You in?"

Kade groaned, the thought of any alcohol turning his stomach. "The PI sent me a picture of Lexie and Julian together," he said, his stomach twisting painfully at the reminder.

Derek muttered a curse. "We'll be right there."

Twenty minutes later, both men arrived and made themselves at home on Kade's couch. They'd already examined the photo.

"I've tried and tried, and I can't come up with one good explanation for it," Kade muttered, and that was only part of the reason he hadn't returned her calls.

"I know it doesn't look good, but you should probably talk to her," Derek said. "I don't see Lexie as someone capable of … what? Corporate espionage? Playing both sides?"

"You just like her," Kade muttered.

"I do too, but he's right. This looks extremely bad," Luke said. "So what are you going to do?"

"Fire her." Kade's stomach twisted into knots as the answer came to him, loud and clear.

Chapter Eleven

L EXIE HAD A crappy weekend. Kendall's headache that wasn't had turned into a raging migraine by Sunday night, which had necessitated a trip to the emergency room for IV meds. She'd tried to call and text Kade more than once, but he wasn't returning her messages, and that wasn't like him.

By the time Monday came, she felt like she hadn't slept much all weekend. Because she hadn't. Between missing Kade, not understanding his silence, and her sister's off-kilter behavior, her own head was spinning.

Although she overslept, she wasn't about to miss work. She piled her hair on top of her head in a messy bun, put on some blush, along with mascara, and rushed out the door, miraculously making it to work before Kade. The minute he stepped out of the elevator, she headed for the coffeemaker and prepared his morning brew the way he liked it and walked over to his office.

"Good morning," she said, entering without knocking. After the weekend she'd had, she couldn't wait to see him.

He stood at his desk, wearing a dark tee shirt and a pair of old jeans. He didn't look up when she spoke, and her stomach pitched uncomfortably.

"Put the coffee down," he said.

"Look, I know I wasn't able to come over Saturday night, and I didn't explain, but I will." She'd decided that it was time to tell him about her sister's battle with mental illness and all the ways it had impacted her life.

"You think that's all you have to explain?" he asked coolly, his gaze cold.

She shivered at the harshness in his tone that she didn't understand. "Kade..."

"Have you seen my watch?" he asked, abruptly changing the subject.

"What?"

"My watch." He tapped his wrist. "The one I keep on my nightstand," he said, his gaze never leaving her face.

She felt scrutinized and uncomfortable, and she folded her arms across her chest in a defensive gesture. "Well, I saw it the last time we were together at your apartment." He liked to touch the surface while he talked. It was part of his morning routine too.

"What about Saturday? When you dropped off the dry cleaning? Did you see it then?"

"No. I went directly to your closet and put away your clothes. Then I threw the plastic into the trash and I left. Why?"

He studied her, his jaw clenched tight.

"Well?"

"Because it's missing."

Her breath left on a harsh exhale. "And you think I *stole* it?" she asked, her voice cracking along with her heart. "How could you accuse me of something like that?"

He strode around the desk, crossing his arms over his chest, mimicking her stance. "Because I know for a fact I saw the timepiece Saturday morning, and you were the only one to enter the apartment between the time I left and when I reached for it the next morning."

Not the only one, she thought, realizing that her sister had not only been with her but she'd entered the bedroom while Lexie was in the closet. Her body went cold, and fear permeated her insides. Oh my God, no wonder Kendall's behavior had changed the minute they'd left Kade's place. Kendall had been antsy and claimed she had a headache and needed to lie down, but instead she'd gone out to meet her new boyfriend. Could he have something to do with her sister *stealing*?

Kendall had her issues, but she'd never resorted to theft. Then again, Lexie didn't know how much money Kendall owed on her recent purchases.

Nausea filled her throat.

"Nothing to say?" Kade asked sarcastically.

"I didn't take the watch," she said, hearing the pleading in her voice. "I swear. But—"

He held up a hand, cutting her off before she could explain. And she was going to do just that. Tell him all about Kendall and beg him not to press charges because her twin was sick and needed help.

"No excuses. I don't want to hear them. This is all I needed to see." He pulled his phone from his back pocket, hit a few buttons, and held it up in front of her eyes.

There, on the screen, was a photo of Kendall, in the same clothes she'd worn Saturday, holding hands with a man who must be her boyfriend. "That's—"

"You and Julian Dane, the man suing me and my partners. I have eyes," Kade said, not withholding the sarcasm.

She let out a sound of distress. "No," she whispered, the pieces of a puzzle she hadn't known she was putting together finally falling into place. Kendall's new boyfriend, *Jay*, was Julian.

"Yes. I know everything. You've been a busy woman, screwing me at the same time you're fucking him," Kade spat.

She flinched at both the ugly accusations and the cold, unfeeling tone of voice. It was as if they'd never been intimate, his body had never been full and thick inside hers.

Dizziness assaulted her, and she fell against the desk, needing something to keep her upright. "It's not me."

Kade frowned. "Like I said, I'm not blind. Get your things and get the fuck out."

"Whoa." Derek walked into the room and slammed the door behind them.

"I can handle this," Kade said.

"I don't think so. The whole office can hear what's going on in here, and you're not normally one to air your dirty laundry."

Lexie pulled herself together and stood up straight. "I have a twin." She cleared her throat.

"What?" Kade spun to face her.

"I have a twin." She spoke louder. "And I know this looks bad on so many levels, but she's sick. I can't explain now but I will. I just have to talk to her first." She had to find out what was going on and whether Kendall was a willing participant in Julian's scheme, or if she was being used as well.

Then, once Kade calmed down, she'd have to convince him not to press charges against her twin. She turned and headed for the exit, opened the door and ran out.

Ignoring the stares of the other employees as she passed, she headed for the elevator and took it downstairs.

She couldn't bring herself to think about the relationship she'd finally allowed herself to have and how it had just crumbled around her. Nor could she begin to process how cruel and mean Kade had been to her, the things he'd thought her capable of. And he'd had good reason to believe them. She couldn't even call his assumptions unreasonable or overreactions.

God, when would her twin stop messing up the things in her life that meant something to her? When Lexie stopped letting her, a small voice inside her said. Lexie understood, but she just wasn't sure she knew how to cut the tie that bound them and let Kendall flounder on her own. And once again, that meant giving up her wants and desires in favor of taking care of her sister.

KADE STARED AT the door Lexie had just run through, stunned by her words. "A twin? A fucking twin?" he asked, feeling as though he had whiplash.

Derek spread his hands in front of him. "I didn't know, man. But what are you doing? Go after her."

Since Kade obviously wasn't capable of thinking for himself, he listened to his best friend and took off after Lexie. He caught up with her downstairs, as she attempted to hail a cab, but because it was still morning rush hour, fate was on Kade's side and they were all full.

"Lexie, wait."

She must have heard his voice because she stilled.

"Lexie."

Slowly, she turned, and the look on her face absolutely gutted him. Pain was evident in her sad eyes and hurt showed in her expression.

"What is it?" she asked. "Because I need to talk to my sister and figure out what's going on. I'll get your watch back somehow and make things right. Just please, please don't call the police?" she asked, begging him on her twin's behalf.

She obviously didn't know why her sister had stolen his watch or how she'd come to be with Julian, but she was going to protect her with every fiber of her being. A big part of Kade admired her for her loyalty in the face of pretty damning evidence. Because at one time he'd had a younger brother who was like a twin to him. One he'd have done anything for.

He exhaled hard. "I'm not calling the police. I just think we should talk too." There was so much he didn't know or understand, and he couldn't just let her go with the ugly words he'd said hanging between them.

"But Kendall—"

He assumed that was her sister's name. "You can talk to her later. Nothing is going to change between now and then. Please." He dug deep for that last word.

Despite now knowing Lexie hadn't betrayed him, he'd spent twenty-four hours thinking she had. And it had been too damned easy for him to believe the worst. He needed to figure out what that said about himself, that he was willing to throw her out without listening to an explanation after the things they'd shared. But first he needed the whole story.

She blew out a long breath. "Okay. I owe you a conversation, at the very least."

He didn't want her here because she owed him, but the truth was he didn't know what he needed or wanted besides an explanation.

They started to walk. "I told you about my mother's depression," she said.

"Yes. And you did mention that you had a sister. You just never said twin."

He glanced her way, but she'd dipped her head, and when she spoke, it was low and difficult to hear. "Sometimes I just want to forget, you know? I want to pretend that my life is normal, that I can have friends and a serious relationship without having to drop everything at a moment's notice because Kendall is bipolar and spiraling out of control. I know better, of course, and today proved it. But for the short time I knew I'd have with you, I wanted it to be about just ... us."

Without thought, he reached over and grabbed her hand, needing to feel her, to be closer, to show her he understood.

"When we got together, I told you my life was complicated and I wasn't looking for anything serious. She's why."

They reached a corner and stopped, waiting for the red light to change to green before crossing and continuing on. They passed people walking dogs, vendors selling pretzels, bagels, and soft-drinks, and life went on as normal in the busy city. Except Kade didn't feel normal anymore.

Everything had done a one-eighty, and given how much he detested change, his insides were churning and panic was setting in. When this was over, losing her was a very real possibility, and that wasn't something he was ready to deal with.

"Listen, now that you understand, I really need to talk to her."

"I'm coming with you," he said, deciding as he spoke.

She came to a halt and turned to face him. "What?

You can't. She'll take one look at you and freak out."

"Or she'll take one look at me and spill her guts. What are the chances she'll tell you everything if you're alone?" he asked, willing himself to ignore the fear in her eyes.

She didn't reply, letting him know he was right. Besides, he wasn't going to hurt her sister. He just wanted answers. More than that, though, he didn't want Lexie to face this alone.

Maybe he was a nicer guy than he'd thought. Or maybe this woman meant more to him than he wanted to believe.

LEXIE'S STOMACH CHURNED as she and Kade took a cab to her apartment. She didn't know what awaited her any more than she understood why he insisted on being there. She could handle her sister. But he did have a point. Kendall was more likely to cave if Kade was there, and she was intimidated by his presence. She didn't have to like it though.

A little while later, she let them into her place, realizing it was the first time Kade had been there. Subconsciously she'd been avoiding allowing her worlds to collide in any way. And that had been a mistake, she realized now. Not just because the distance she'd created had allowed Kendall to run amok in Kade's life, the very opposite of Lexie's intentions, but because what kind of relationship could they have had if she didn't share everything?

She pursed her lips at that thought and stepped inside.

"Kendall?" she called out. She'd left her sister at home in bed this morning, recovering from the migraine. She'd said she had no plans to leave the apartment. "Kendall?"

"What's with all the racket?" Her twin stepped out of her room wearing an old sleep shirt and a pair of sweats. "Oh! Who's this?" she asked, pushing her hair out of her eyes and looking Kade over, appreciation in her gaze.

Lexie drew a deep breath, aware of his large, looming presence behind her. "Kendall, this is my ... boss, Kaden Barnes," she said, deliberately keeping things professional. "Kade, this is my sister, Kendall."

"Nice to meet you," Kade said, stepping up beside Lexie.

Her twin's eyes popped open wide. "Oh. Hi. Well, then, I'll just leave you two alone." She spun around with the obvious intention of closing herself back in her room.

"Kendall, we need to talk to you," Lexie said.

Her sister's steps slowed. "I'm not feeling well," she mumbled without turning back to face them.

"I'm sure you're not," Lexie murmured.

Kade put a hand on her shoulder, and despite the absurdity of the entire situation, she appreciated his attempt to support her.

"Come on, Kendall. Let's all sit down," Lexie insisted.

Shoulders slumped, Kendall followed them over to the couch, and they all settled in, Kade in the big club chair in the corner.

"Kade, really, I can talk to her alone," Lexie tried once more.

"No." He remained in his seat, but he didn't attempt to lead the conversation, allowing Lexie to jump in.

"Kendall, what do you know about your boyfriend?" Lexie opted to start with a broad question and not an accusation. She'd get there. Somehow.

"Jay?" Kendall asked, clearly startled by the subject. "I told you. We met at the gym. He's been good to me. Well, until yesterday," she muttered. "Haven't heard from him since I saw him on Saturday, and he hasn't replied to my texts about being in the hospital on Saturday night," she said, obviously hurt by his neglect.

Lexie shot Kade a concerned glance.

"What's Jay's last name?" Kade asked her.

"Dane. Why?"

"I'll explain in a minute." Lexie closed her eyes and shook her head, wishing she'd asked that question sooner. Still, there was no telling whether she'd have made the connection.

Now for the tougher question. "Did you steal—take—Kade's watch off his dresser yesterday?" Lexie asked.

"What? How could you even ask me that?" Kendall jumped up from her seat, hurt in her eyes. "Lexie, really? You're accusing me of stealing?"

"Sit down," Kade said, speaking up for the first time. "And have some respect for your sister by telling the truth. If you don't want me to call the cops, you'll talk to us."

"Kade!" Lexie didn't want him attacking her twin.

"Pussyfooting around isn't going to solve anything. Kendall, did you take the watch?" he asked her.

Her sister's shoulders slumped again. "Yes, okay? I overspent on a credit card and—"

"I thought you cut up all your cards," Lexie interrupted.

"Yeah, well, I got another one," Kendall said without meeting Lexie's gaze. "And things got out of control. You won't give me more than the bare necessities to live. Dad wouldn't help me out. I was desperate. Jay said you wouldn't miss it if I took a little something," Kendall said, shaking as she spoke.

She lowered herself back into her seat, head hung low.

"How did Jay know anything about Kade at all?" Lexie asked.

"He asked a lot of questions about you," Kendall said to Lexie. "He wanted to get to know me better and was interested in my family. Why is that a problem?" she asked defensively.

"When?" Kade asked. "When did he start asking questions?"

Kendall met his gaze. "After your picture showed up on Page Six with Lexie."

"Fuck," Kade muttered.

"What?" Kendall asked.

Lexie glanced at him, waiting for him to explain.

Kade rubbed his finger over the casing of his watch. "I'm going to assume Julian had someone watching me. Someone who knew about us before the gala. Probably after you spent the night that first time after my accident." He held up his injured hand. "I'm sure he looked into you," he said to Lexie. "It's what I would have done. Hell, it's what I was doing and how I found out about Julian and Kendall," Kade muttered. "And Julian probably introduced himself to your sister right after the PI gave him the info."

"Who is this Julian?" Kendall asked, perplexed and wary.

Lexie slid closer to her sister and put an arm around her shoulder. Because no matter what Kendall had done, she was her twin, and this news was going to hurt. "Julian is Jay's real name. And Julian is suing Kade for a piece of his company. I'm sorry, honey, but he was using you to get to Kade through me."

Kendall met her gaze, identical watery blue eyes staring back at her. "He *used* me? He set me up from the beginning?"

Lexie nodded.

"What happened after he saw the Page Six picture?" Kade asked.

"He started talking about how much money Kade must have, and when I said I had financial problems, he told me if I took something from the apartment, a guy like Kade had so much he would never miss it. He suggested it often, and I was desperate enough to do it." She pulled at her sweats over and over. "I got myself in deep and I kept spending. I hit my limit but the bill was coming in." She started to cry. "I didn't mean to steal. Jay said it wouldn't hurt anyone, and I wanted to believe it."

Lexie pulled her twin against her, looking at Kade over her sister's trembling body. "I'm going to kill him," she muttered.

"Not if I get to him first. Kendall," Kade said in a gentler voice, "you said you haven't heard from him since Saturday. What happened Saturday?"

"I gave him the watch to pawn, and he said he'd get me the money. He hasn't gotten back to me. He always answers right away, and now it's like he's disappeared." She sniffed and pulled away. "I feel so stupid."

"Don't. He set you up and used you. There's no way you could have known."

"I'll find Julian and take care of things," Kade said, rising from his seat.

"Wait. I stole from you," Kendall said, her voice rising, as if realizing what she'd done for the first time. "Oh my God. Are you going to call the police?" She jumped up in a panic.

Lexie rose to her feet too. "Kade said he wouldn't," she told her sister, looking to him for reassurance.

He nodded, indicating he planned to keep his promise, and she breathed a long sigh of relief. He paused, as if waiting for her to say something more, but she was spent, lost, and hurting. And Kendall was silently sobbing in relief, hanging on to Lexie with everything she had.

Kade gave her one long, lingering look. "I'll just let myself out," he finally said.

"Thank you," she mouthed at him.

One side of his mouth lifted in a small smile before he turned and walked out.

Kendall collapsed then, dissolving into a heap on the floor, consumed by huge, gulping sobs. So Lexie did what she always did; she knelt down and took care of her twin, pushing aside the fact that this whole mess had affected her life too.

She'd lost her job and a guy she really cared about because Kendall had once again spiraled out of control.

Chapter Twelve

KADE KNEW HE had to make decisions about a lot of things in his life, starting with Julian. It was unacceptable that he'd go after anyone in Kade's life, let alone target a woman who'd never done anything to him. Worse, a woman with a mental illness who would never have seen him coming. Kade didn't just want to stand up for Lexie, he wanted to look out for her sister.

Instead of going to work the next morning, he headed for Julian's apartment in Midtown. He walked up the stairs of the old brownstone building, his temper rising as he reached the apartment and knocked hard on the door. He timed his visit before nine a.m., hoping to catch Julian at home and, yeah, maybe at a weak moment. Who knew what he'd been doing the night before. For damn sure he hadn't been with Kendall.

When no one answered, he banged harder. "Julian, open the fucking door."

Just when he thought he was going to have to turn around and come back later, the door swung open, and his old friend stood in front of him. This was the same guy he'd met freshman year and bonded with from day one. Julian had spent holidays with Kade and his father when his parents couldn't be bothered. But at some point, drugs had become more important than friendship, and nothing had been the same since.

"Can I help you?" Julian greeted him, arms folded across his chest, dressed for the day in a pair of jeans and a white tee shirt and surprisingly clear-eyed.

Kade brushed past him and walked into his apartment. No way he wanted to have this out in the hall. He waited until Julian shut the door behind him before confronting him.

"I'm here so we can have this out between us. Because only a coward hides behind a woman."

"You figured that one out, huh? I have to admit it was fun getting one over on you. Did you think I was fucking your girlfriend?"

Kade was too aware of his already fractured knuckles to haul off and punch his former friend. "I'm really glad that gets you off, buddy. Too bad the woman you hurt has other issues. Good job, asshole."

Julian flinched, and a telltale muscle twitched near

his left eye. A sure sign he hadn't done his homework on Kendall Parker before he'd seduced her and set her up.

"What are you talking about?" Julian asked.

Kade wasn't about to give away private information. "Nothing you need to worry about now that you used her, dumped her, and she's completely aware of what a prick you are."

"I didn't mean to hurt her," Julian said, his voice low, looking and sounding more like the man Kade used to know. "She seemed like she was up for a good time."

"Yeah, well, you never were the best judge of character. Where's my watch?"

"Gone. I pawned it."

No shock there, Kade thought. "And the cash? God knows you didn't give it to Kendall to help pay her debts."

Julian didn't reply. Again, Kade wasn't surprised. He hadn't come here expecting to get anything back.

"It was never about the money. I just wanted you to know I could get to you. Mission accomplished," Julian said, sounding smug and pleased with himself.

"What do you want?" Kade asked. "What's it going to take for you to go away?"

"Finally, he sees reason." Julian's eyes flashed dollar signs. The greedy bastard obviously thought Kade was here to cave. "Given what I've got on you, I want one-quarter of Blink's net worth. I was there when the four of us came up with the idea together, and I'm going to profit like the rest of you."

Kade shook his head. "You were drunk and high when we came up with the idea. No way are you taking close to that amount."

"Maybe you're forgetting I've got Lila. I can blow your cushy life sky-high." Julian's grin exuded overconfidence, and that would be his downfall. "I own you," Julian said.

"That's where you're wrong." Kade pushed past him, heading for the door. "Nobody owns me but me." And he knew just what to do to prove it to himself once and for all.

Lexie couldn't get out of bed. She wanted to. She needed to pick herself up and move forward, but she decided she needed time to mourn the relationship she'd had, however briefly. Kade had brought something to her life she hadn't known she needed. She'd spent so much time taking care of her sister and putting her own needs aside she'd almost forgotten she had desires that most women took for granted.

For a short time, she'd enjoyed being the focus of a man's attention. And not just any man. Kaden

Barnes had shown up in her life and turned it upside down. He was unique on so many levels. Intelligent to a degree she couldn't come close to comprehending. His arrogance was a cover for insecurities over things he couldn't control. His ADHD, his anxiety, all things that were a part of what made him unique and defined him also set him apart from others.

She was pretty sure he had his mother to thank for making him feel those things made him less than … less than his brother. Less than a man. Ironically, those were the qualities she found his most endearing. He was also generous and giving despite being hurt over and over. He could so easily have pressed charges against her sister. God only knew what that watch cost. But he hadn't and she'd be forever grateful to him.

Kade deserved a woman who could embrace those things that made him unique, which she did, and be there for him one hundred percent, which she obviously could not. No matter how much she loved him, and she did.

She loved him in a way her younger self couldn't have imagined, and she wanted to give him everything. But she was pulled in two different directions, the twin she loved, who had no one else by her side, ever present. Always demanding.

As if on cue, a knock sounded on her bedroom

door. After Kade had left, she and her sister had both retreated to their own rooms. They'd eaten dinner separately, each alone with their thoughts. Lexie hadn't been ready to deal with her sister, and she suspected Kendall had been too upset and humiliated by everything Julian had done to face Lexie.

Apparently Kendall was ready now.

"Come in," Lexie called out, bracing to deal with her sister. She pushed herself upright in bed as Kendall walked in, looking no better than Lexie felt.

She still wore the same sleep clothes she'd been in when she'd met Kade yesterday, her hair was a tangled mess, and her eyes were red-rimmed from crying. Lexie had a feeling she was looking in the mirror.

"Can I sit down?" Kendall asked softly.

Lexie nodded. "Are you okay?" she asked.

"Not really." Kendall eased herself onto the bed and folded her legs beneath her.

"I'm sorry about Julian. You never should have been targeted by that bastard."

Kendall shrugged. "I shouldn't have done the things I did either. I knew I wasn't feeling right. I knew the meds Dr. Kay switched me to weren't working, but I was riding the high. I'm the one who got myself in debt. I'm the one who stole Kade's watch. It wasn't Julian who did those things. It was me." Her voice caught as she choked on a sob.

Lexie wanted to pull her twin into her arms, but she understood this was a breakthrough and Kendall needed to have it. So she waited for her sister to pull herself together and to go on.

Kendall shivered and wrapped her arms around herself. "I'm so sorry," she said, rocking back and forth. "I'm humiliated, and I don't like the person I've become. I'm so lucky your boyfriend is such a decent guy or I'd be in jail right now."

Lexie expelled a long breath, grateful her twin was coming to these realizations on her own. She met Kendall's gaze. "He's not my boyfriend," she said, correcting that misconception.

"But I thought you two were involved."

"We were. Until he accused me of stealing and betraying him with Julian."

Get the fuck out.

She shivered at the memory of his cold, accusatory tone and how he'd thrown her out of his office as if she meant nothing to him.

"Oh my God. That's my fault too." Kendall looked up at Lexie with big, watery eyes. "I'm sure you can fix things. He knows it wasn't you, and he isn't pressing charges against me. That's got to be because of you. Because he loves you."

Lexie shook her head hard. Love? She was pretty sure he considered himself well rid of her. She brought complications no man in his right mind needed in his life. Because of his relationship with her, he'd ended up vulnerable to Julian's manipulations.

"Don't worry about me," Lexie murmured. "Let's talk about you."

Her sister let out a harsh laugh. "What about me? I think I've hit the proverbial rock bottom." She looked away. "I called Dr. Kay and told him I wanted to check myself into an inpatient facility and get help."

"Kendall!"

"Long term, this time. Not a two-week-and-I'm-out sort of deal. I have to learn to function on my own. To find the right cocktail of meds, to have the correct therapy. I can't go on like this anymore. The ups and downs are killing me, and worse, they're hurting you, and I'm so, so tired of hurting too." Her sister's rocking continued as she broke down in gulping, loud sobs.

Lexie couldn't believe her sister was finally reaching out for real long-term help. Admiration welled up inside her.

She crawled over the bed and grabbed her twin, hugging her tight. "It'll be okay," she murmured. "I'm so proud of you. So proud. And I'll be by your side the whole time. You can do this. I know you can." She stroked her sister's hair and whispered comforting words in her ear, doing all the things a mother would do. If only they had a capable mother.

Kendall held on to her as she cried like a little girl while Lexie choked back her own tears. Tears for her twin, for the hard life Kendall had, and for Lexie's own choices and losses.

For Kade, the man who meant everything to her. And the man she had to let go.

KADE SHOULDN'T HAVE been surprised when Lexie didn't show up for work the next morning. He'd fired her. Not just fired her. He'd told her to *get the fuck out*. Despite all that had gone down with her twin sister yesterday, he hadn't asked her to come back to him. Not as his PA and not as his woman.

The PA had been a mistake. On a professional level, he needed her to keep things running smoothly. She was always two steps ahead of him and the perfect assistant for a man like him.

Coming back to *him*, that was another story. Without a doubt, he knew he wanted and needed her in his life, by his side for the long haul. But he was about to make some extremely drastic moves, and he didn't think it was fair to ask her to stand by his side as he made them.

"Kade." Luke walked into his office, Derek right behind him.

"Shut the door," Kade said, walking around his desk and joining his friends.

"I don't know why. You don't have an assistant to overhear anything," Derek said, his sarcastic tone indicating he wasn't happy with Kade.

He got it. He wasn't happy with how he'd treated Lexie in this very room yesterday either. He still had to apologize for that, and would when he explained why she no longer had a job. He didn't want her thinking she was fired. It was more complicated than that. But this meeting had to come first. When all was said and done, he might not have a position for her to return to.

"Let's sit," Kade said, easing himself onto the edge of his desk, facing his friends.

Derek and Luke eyed him suspiciously as they settled into their chairs.

"What's going on?"

Kade cleared his throat. "First you should know I admire the hell out of you two. You're my brothers, and there's nothing I wouldn't do for you. Which is why I'm pulling out of Blink."

Derek was out of his seat, but Luke, ever the more rational and calm when it came to personal decisions, pulled him back.

"Let him explain," Luke said.

"I went to see Julian. He's not going to back down

until he gets what he wants, and he's demanding one quarter of what we've built." He curled his good hand around the desk. "No fucking way will I let that happen."

"You know we can fight him," Derek said.

"And we're willing to go all the way." This from Luke.

Kade shook his head. "That's why you're my brothers. That's also why I won't let you. He's proven he's willing to play dirty and hurt people who don't deserve it. People who won't see him coming and aren't capable of fighting back."

"Lexie," Derek said.

Kade nodded. "And her twin. Her sister is bipolar," he said, trusting these two men with the truth. "And that bastard used her and dumped her like yesterday's trash." He couldn't get Lexie's face out his mind, the concern for her sister, the fear in her eyes aimed at him. "I won't add to that."

Derek groaned. "Let's take a breath and regroup."

Kade shook his head. "I called a tech mag reporter I like and trust. I'm telling the truth about my past and signing over my shares of Blink evenly between the two of you. I'm taking away Julian's power to destroy Blink." And to destroy his best friends and their legacy.

"Fuck no." Derek rose and Luke did the same.

"For the record, I agree. You are every bit as much a part of this as we are," Luke said.

Kade rolled his tight shoulders and smiled at his friends. "I appreciate that. But it's my past threatening the empire. I'm going to handle it the only way I know how." Ironically he was at peace with his decision. "Just promise me one thing."

"Anything, man. You know that," Derek said.

"When you settle with Julian, and the lawyers already said he's going to get something if we go to court, make sure it's the bare minimum and no part of the company."

Luke pulled him into a brotherly hug. "I admire the hell out of you."

Kade slapped the other man on the back, then turned to Derek.

"Are you sure there's no other way?" Derek asked. "Like admitting to the Lila situation and we ride out the storm together?"

He shook his head. "I made some calls, spoke to some investors, and if I stick around, the IPO goes up in flames. But even more importantly, I won't let him go after anyone else we care about, and if I remain a part of Blink, my gut tells me he'll keep coming."

"This sucks," Derek muttered.

Kade grinned. "There are worse things in life than losing billions."

Like losing the woman he loved.

LEXIE SAT WITH the computer open to Indeed and Monster.com, looking for a job. Kendall was at a therapy appointment, and Waffles was asleep at her feet. In another open window on her computer, she worked on her resume. She hoped Kade would give her a recommendation, although she knew it didn't look good to have held her last job for a mere couple of weeks, and for the one before that, she lacked references. She didn't think Kade would be looking to hurt her professionally, although deep down she knew she didn't deserve anything from him at all. He'd already given her the biggest gift he could, not reporting her sister to the police.

As she narrowed her search choices, she decided to stick with secretarial and professional-assistant-type jobs, knowing, at the very least, that's where her skills lay. Once she had her sister situated inpatient somewhere, she could apply for a job without worrying about Kendall wreaking havoc, at least until she was released.

Lexie sighed and went back to looking. She didn't know how long she'd been at it when the doorbell rang. Maybe Kendall had forgotten her keys. She strode over and opened the door.

"Kade!" He was the last person she expected to see, and damned if her heart didn't pick up speed at the sight of him.

In his khaki pants and green Army shirt, he was every inch the sexy tech god she adored. She pushed back the flood of desire, knowing it had no place between them. Not anymore.

"What are you doing here?" she asked.

"Can we talk?"

She deliberately squelched the spark of hope in her chest because nothing had changed. She'd decided that earlier today. "Of course."

Waffles jumped up on his hind legs, his front paws on Kade's jeans, begging for attention. "Hey, buddy." He petted the dog's head, talking to him in silly tones that made Lexie smile and warmth fill her at the sight. Of course he would be good with dogs too.

"His name is Waffles," she said.

Kade groaned. "Thanks to who?"

"My sister." Lexie laughed. "I suppose you'd have a manlier name for a dog?"

He shrugged. "Never gave it much thought. I didn't have a pet growing up."

"Maybe you should get one now. Dogs are soothing."

He glanced at the furry thing still begging for attention. "I'll take your word for it."

She hoped he'd consider it. There were therapy pets meant just for people with anxiety and other unique needs, and she wanted to know he had company at night. Furry canine company would be her preference, but she also wanted him to have a full and happy life. She didn't want to consider just what that meant.

"Come sit." She led him into the family room, and they settled beside each other on the sofa. "We're alone, in case you're wondering. Kendall is at a doctor's appointment, so feel free to talk." She gestured around the empty apartment.

"I wanted to discuss your job. Things are changing at Blink, and I won't be needing an assistant."

He didn't elaborate, and she didn't ask, no longer feeling like it was her business to push him for answers. It hurt her, that she could no longer speak her mind or know what was in the deeper recesses of his.

Still, she appreciated him letting her know in person, considering he'd already technically fired her. "Don't worry about me. I was looking for a job before you got here. See?" She pointed to the open laptop on the ottoman in front of them.

He frowned at the screen. "You don't need to worry about employment ads. I promised you that no matter what happened between us, you'd have a job at Blink. Whenever you're ready, go back and Derek will have a position for you."

She blinked back tears. "Kade, I don't deserve that kind of generosity. Kendall shouldn't have been in your apartment. She shouldn't have had the chance to take your watch in the first place. That's on me."

He shook his head, his gaze warm and understanding. "Julian being able to get close to your sister? That's on *me*. So maybe we call it even?"

"Yeah. Even sounds good." Maybe she could say good-bye knowing he didn't hate her for how things had turned out between them. Heaven knew she didn't hate him.

He reached out and touched her hair, curling one strand around his fingers. "I'm glad I had you in my life for a little while, because in that short time, you taught me a lot."

"I did?" She couldn't imagine what.

He nodded. "You're everything I never had in my life. You're loyal, caring, honest. You accept people for who they are, and you're there for the people who need you. You were there for me."

Because she loved him.

She reached up and clasped his wrist, pulling his hand down and holding on. "You deserve someone who can do that for you. Someone who can give you one hundred percent, and that's not me right now. It may never be me."

"I'm selfish enough to want to pull you away from your twin, but I'm smart enough to know who needs you more. I wish I'd had someone who was there for me when I needed them, so I won't ask you to choose." He pulled her close, resting his forehead against hers.

She sighed, breathing in his masculine scent, soaking in as much as she could of him in this short time she had left. It wasn't a lot and it wasn't nearly enough.

So she was surprised when his lips trailed down her cheek. Unable to help herself, she tilted her head, giving him a silent okay for his lips to press against hers. And when they did, there was no doubt the chemistry between them was still strong. Just as there was no doubt this was an emotional moment, one she wanted to drink in and remember.

She wrapped her arms around his neck, and he pulled her close, until she straddled him on the sofa, sex soft and needy against his thickening erection. He slid his tongue into her mouth, and she moaned, reveling in what she sensed was a good-bye neither was ready to accept.

A smarter woman would break things off now, but she wanted this. She wanted him, and if it was the last time, she was going to commit every moment to memory. His tongue glided against hers, eradicating brain cells with every touch, tangle, and sweep throughout her mouth.

She edged her lower body closer. He grabbed her waist, holding her down as she rocked her hips, letting desire and waves of passion build between them.

He pulled back suddenly, meeting her gaze. "Bedroom?"

He was asking permission, not wanting to overstep. There was no way he could. In answer, she threaded her fingers through his short hair, sliding them against his scalp.

With a groan, he rose, lifting her along with him.

She wrapped her legs around his waist, helping take her weight off him as he made his way through the room and to the small hallway. "Far door at the end."

He followed her instructions and she turned the knob. He walked her in, kicking the door shut behind them. He laid her on the bed and yanked his tee shirt over his head, revealing his bare, muscled chest. She'd reached for her top, but she'd rather watch him undress than get herself to that particular state.

His gaze never leaving hers, he kicked off his shoes. His khakis and boxers followed. Next thing she knew, he stood over her, completely naked, his hot, hard erection standing at attention.

Her sex softened, and moisture trickled into her underwear, desire for this man and the pleasure he could bring her overwhelming. Knowing this was their swan song only made things more bittersweet, and she wanted to savor it. He reached for her, hooking his fingers into the waistband of her sweats—minus the splint, she noticed—and pulled them down and off. She rid herself of her tank top and quickly shed her bra, until she was as naked as he was.

And because of the intimacy they'd already shared, she had no embarrassment lying bare before him, only a deep yearning to feel him pulsing inside her, his gorgeous gaze focused on her as he thrust in and out of her soaking-wet sex.

He leaned over, bracing one knee on the mattress, and splayed his hand over her lower belly, his gaze hot on her breasts, lowering to her pussy.

"You're so fucking beautiful," he said in a reverent voice she'd never heard from him before, and a swell of emotion rose in her throat.

His hand, a hot brand on her belly, slid downward, his fingers grazing her outer lips, gliding over the moisture gathered there just for him. He slid one finger inside her, swirling around, arousing her beyond reason.

She shook as he pumped in, then pulled out and held up his glistening finger. "I think you're wet for me," he said, licking her taste off his finger with a satisfied moan.

She'd always be wet for him, she mused, keeping that thought to herself.

"Please tell me you have a condom," she said. "Because I don't keep them on hand."

A pleased smile lifted his lips. "I'm so glad to hear that. I think I have one in my wallet. I stuck one in there after we started ... you know."

She was pleased that, but for her, he didn't make a habit of carrying them on him.

"But I'm not ready for that yet. I like tasting you too much." He spread her knees apart with his hands, leaned down, and blew a warm breath on her aching sex.

"Kade." Her hips rose from the bed, and he answered her silent plea by pulling her clit into his mouth.

No slow foreplay, no licking and teasing, just an immediate rush for the goal. He nipped at the engorged bud, and waves of pleasure rose, her entire being focused on that tiny place that was bringing such great sensation. He licked and tugged, grazed her with his teeth, until her hips were bucking, and she was grinding against him in search of relief.

"Oh God." She cried out, unaware of the words coming from her lips.

He pushed one finger up inside her, then added a second, and the fullness, along with the pressure on her clit, caused her to shatter.

"Ooh, I'm coming. Kade!" Her orgasm hit, sweeping her to a place of pure pleasure, as waves of ecstasy washed over her.

He stayed with her throughout, licking her clit and easing up slowly, bringing her down. Then he leaned over and grabbed his wallet, pulling out the condom and covering himself in record time.

He met her gaze, a somewhat melancholy smile on his lips, one she didn't have time to process, when he thrust into her body, and suddenly the nerve endings she'd thought were exhausted returned to life.

"Oh, baby, you feel so fucking good," he said through clenched teeth, just as the head of his cock hit a soft spot inside her that had her seeing stars.

Another orgasm hovered, seconds away, as he plunged deep and withdrew, plunged and withdrew, her entire body lost in both his rhythm and the climax that overtook her and didn't seem to want to end.

He began to thrust fast, his sexy face contorted with pleasure. "Fuck. Lexie. *Love you.*"

He came with a long, hard groan, and she wrapped her arms around him, holding on for all she was worth as he trembled and thrust, riding out and prolonging his pleasure.

He collapsed on top of her, causing her breathing to hitch. She didn't care. She wanted to absorb him into her skin, to take everything she could from this one last time.

He finally rolled off her and rose, quickly disposing of the condom before rejoining her in bed.

He wrapped his arms around her and pulled her sated body against his, his words echoing in her mind. *Lexie. Love you. Love you.* The words circled, everything she'd ever wanted to hear. Everything she needed. Nothing she could accept.

Her breathing fell into a synced rhythm with his, and she couldn't help when her eyes grew heavy and she fell asleep in his arms.

When she woke up, he was gone.

Chapter Thirteen

A FEW DAYS after Kade had *made love* to Lexie for both the first and last time, he gave an interview to a print magazine, laying out the details of his past, the secrets he was hiding, and his decision to walk away from Blink.

A week later, he adjusted the tie he wasn't used to wearing and paced the Green Room of one of the big national morning shows. Apparently the world thought he was on the level of Facebook's Zuckerberg or Snapchat's Evan Spiegel. Kade thought it was bullshit, but they were interested in his story. The lawyers and PR people thought it would make for good publicity.

Kade wasn't a guy who wore his heart on his sleeve. He'd gone back to being a complete and utter ass, more because he was upset he'd lost Lexie than for any other reason. That and without Blink to go into every day, he was bored and overly focused on things that were doing him no good.

Like counting tiles on the ceiling as he sat in his doctor's office for a final set of X-rays on his hand and again here, while waiting to go live on air. And obsessively searching for a watch to replace the Patek he'd lost to Julian because nothing else he found felt quite the same. He'd hired Evan Mann to hunt around local pawn shops to find his watch, and the man had come through. He'd had to pay to get his beloved timepiece back, but he had it on his wrist, and that was all that mattered.

"Mr. Barnes, we need to get you mic'ed up."

He blew out a long breath, rose, and followed the intern to the studio. He settled into the chair across from the morning show host and prepared to speak the truth. It wasn't the same as talking to a tech reporter who spoke his language.

This was going to be harder.

More complicated.

More emotional.

And he only hoped he didn't make an ass of himself on national television.

LEXIE SAT IN the waiting room while the attendants at Maple Hill checked her sister into the residential treatment center three hours from home. She and Kendall had driven up yesterday and stayed in a hotel last night. They'd rented a movie and munched on junk food like when they were little. Lexie was happy to have had a good night with her sister before leaving her alone in this place for God knew how long. Treatment plans took a while to formulate, and the center prided itself on a multipronged approach. In other words, her twin would be here awhile.

Lexie was waiting to see Kendall's room and say good-bye. She paced the floor, a morning show droning on in the background. She didn't pay attention to the screen hanging on the wall until a familiar voice sounded in her ear.

"Thank you for having me," Kade said to the pretty blonde morning show host.

He was clean-shaven and wore an expensive-looking suit that defined his well-cut body, and his green eyes were focused on the woman he spoke to. But Lexie's gaze was drawn to his hand. He'd pushed up his sleeve, and he ran his hand over the face of a watch.

His watch. He'd somehow gotten it back. And this interview was causing him stress if he'd chosen to wear it there. Her heart twisted, even as she wondered what he was doing on television.

"Thank you for doing this exclusive interview, a

follow-up to the article written about you in *Wired Magazine*," the woman said.

"You're welcome," he said stiffly.

"This is your first live interview since you revealed the fact that you were accused of date rape when you were in college."

Lexie flinched, shocked at the public conversation.

A muscle twitched in his jaw. "Falsely accused."

"Yes. And we'll get to that in a moment." The woman leaned in closer. "I wanted to ask you first, why did you make the accusations public now and step away from any association with Blink, the company and app you helped put on the map?"

"What?" Lexie shouted at the screen, grateful it was early and she was alone in the waiting room. *He'd* made that awful accusation public? Why?

Kade ran his hand down his freshly shaven face. "Because the company is on the verge of a huge IPO, and this is the kind of information and potential scandal that can ruin the business and hurt my partners and friends."

Kade squared his shoulders and met her gaze, but the way the camera focused, Lexie felt like he was looking directly at her when he answered. "I wanted to take the power away from anyone threatening to use it against me or the people I love."

She let out a small cry, memories of him buried

inside her body and saying those words to *her* surfacing now. Suddenly it became clear. One of the reasons he'd walked away from Blink, the company he loved and had created, was because of her. Julian had used Kade's weaknesses against him, and she had been one of those weaknesses. Because he loved her.

And that's why he'd walked away after they'd made love. So she didn't have to choose between her twin, who needed her, and the man she loved. Not that she'd told him as much.

God, what was wrong with her? He needed her too. And it was about damned time she stood up for herself and what she needed. She needed Kade, and she wanted to be by his side while he was going through this hard time. She wanted to support him and to take care of him.

She opened her purse and searched for her cell phone because she had changes that needed to be made.

"On that note, I have a surprise guest who has something she'd like to say to you," the woman interviewing Kade said.

Lexie stiffened and, holding the phone in her hand, lowered herself into a seat, her gaze glued to the screen.

A woman about Kade's age walked across the stage.

"What the hell is this?" Kade sprung to his feet, fury evident in his expression. "I didn't sign up for an ambush."

"Mr. Barnes, I assure you, this is no such thing. Lila Mills has something she wants to say to you."

Lila. The woman who'd accused him of date rape? Lexie's stomach churned at the drama unfolding.

"Ms. Mills, you called us shortly after this interview with Mr. Barnes was announced. Can you tell Mr. Barnes and our audience why?"

The attractive brunette smoothed her skirt and met Kade's gaze head on. "I wanted to apologize for accusing you all those years ago and to state publicly that you didn't rape me. What happened was consensual."

Lexie blinked, glued to the screen, as, she was certain, was the rest of the audience.

Kade's eyes opened wide. "In other words, you lied."

"Yes." She ducked her head, clearly ashamed.

"Why are you coming forward now?" the host asked.

Lila swallowed hard, her cheeks a deep red. "Back when it happened, I was petrified of my father's anger. I came home late, past curfew, and he could tell immediately what I'd been doing. It was easier to agree when he asked if I'd been forced."

And then you took money to keep quiet, Lexie thought, disgusted.

"What about a few weeks ago when Julian Dane looked you up and asked you if you'd come forward if he needed you?" Kade leaned forward in his seat, pressing the woman. "You were only too happy to go against me again."

Lila glanced down at her hands. "I know. He offered me a lot of money, and God knows, I'm broke. But … when I heard you'd given up your company and walked away from everything to do right by your friends … I couldn't live with myself any longer. I couldn't continue to lie." She shook her head, tears in her eyes.

Real or forced, Lexie didn't know. Lila had vindicated Kade. That's all Lexie knew, heard, or cared about.

With shaking hands, Lexie returned her focus to her phone and dialed, getting her father on the line. "Dad?"

"Lexie, is your sister settled?" he asked.

"Almost, but…" She drew a deep breath. "You need to be here. Kendall is your daughter and I … I have somewhere else I have to be," she said, painful guilt lodging in her chest.

"Lexie, you know I can't leave your mother," her father said, his tone adding to her shame in asking for her own life.

She blinked back tears, forcing out the words that should have been said a long time ago. "No, it's not that you *can't* leave Mom, it's that you won't. There's a difference."

Stunned silence ensued, so Lexie continued.

"You can get full-time help or find a good place where Mom will have the best care. But once I say good-bye to Kendall today, I'm finished being her full-time caregiver, Dad. I can't do it anymore." The weight on her shoulders was still leaden and painful.

She felt guilty, but she knew she had a right to her own life. She'd always be there for her twin, help her if she needed it. But she couldn't put her before Kade. Not if she wanted a life with him. And there was nothing she wanted more.

Assuming Kade still wanted her.

OVER A WEEK had passed since Lexie had seen Kade on morning television and laid down the law with her father. To her surprise, he'd taken a step back and realized the burden he'd put on his daughter. He'd immediately gotten busy interviewing live-in aides in order to keep her mother comfortable at home. Lexie gave him that time, remaining available to her sister, visiting twice a week. She didn't want to pull too far back until her father could really take over. After-wards, Lexie would visit as often as she could reasonably do so. She'd never abandon her twin.

She just wanted time to live her own life.

As for the man she wanted to live it with?

The end result of the interview on the morning show was that Kade did not have to walk away from Blink, and he'd gone back to work. Social media had gone crazy after Lila's admission about her lies. A firestorm of coverage resulted on why it was so difficult for women who'd been raped to be *heard* in today's society. Because of lies like Lila's, true victims were afraid they wouldn't be believed.

Kade had stepped forward to help change that. Despite being wrongly accused, he'd donated a sub-stantial amount of money to RAINN, the Rape Abuse & Incest National Network, also known for running the National Sexual Assault Hotline in order to help women who have been victims of rape. He was everyone's hero.

He'd always been hers.

How did she go about proving to the man who had everything that she loved him and wanted to put him first? Lexie put her brain to work and came up with two things she could do to make her point.

She was going to return to work as his assistant. Invited or not, expected or not, he needed someone who understood him, and Lexie was it. Even if he no longer wanted a relationship with her, she intended to stand by him and do her job. Because she knew how well they clicked and how much she helped him manage day-to-day living.

Her second idea was more complicated and risky, but she'd taken care of that too. He'd either be thrilled or he'd never forgive her. Either way, she was going to be around to see the end result.

So now, on another rainy Monday, with her father visiting Kendall at the treatment center, Lexie dressed for work. She was nervous, not knowing what kind of reception she'd receive at Blink. Maybe Kade would be happy to see her. Maybe he'd written her off for good. She wouldn't know until she showed up there.

Of course, Waffles, who was now her responsibility, chose this morning to get sick, necessitating a messy cleanup and a change of clothes, causing Lexie to be late getting out of the apartment. She'd hired a dog walker and had to leave the young girl a note, letting her know to watch out for the dog's upset stomach, then ran for the bus. In a *Groundhog's Day* repeat of her first day at work, she also forgot her umbrella and was splattered with rain by the time she got onto the bus.

In other words, there was no way she was going to make a good impression on her surprise return to the office.

★   ★   ★

KADE STRODE INTO his private office and glanced out the wall-to-wall windows and into the gloomy rain that matched his mood. Despite the weather, he ought to be happy because, at the very least, he had part of his life back. Blink, his baby, the thing that defined him, was his, and he was no longer forced to walk away. That, in and of itself, was a relief because he'd put his lifeblood into the company.

Hell, it was all he had since losing Lexie.

"Good morning, Mr. Barnes," a chipper, *familiar* voice said.

He blinked in surprise, his pulse picking up speed. As if his thoughts had conjured her, Lexie popped up from beneath his desk. Her hair was pulled into a high ponytail, and she had rain stains on her white shirt, which was tucked into that black pencil skirt he loved.

Déjà vu, he thought, hope racing through his veins as she adjusted the computer on the desk.

"What are you doing?" he asked, as curious as he was pleased to see her.

"Well, let's see. Someone moved your computer back to where it was before I changed things around."

He shrugged. "That would be the cleaning staff. They came in and did a mass dusting and cleaning."

He'd arrived the next morning to discover nothing was where he'd left it. "I fired them right after."

A smile lifted the corners of her mouth. "Well, you're all fixed now."

"I can see that." His desk was back to its neat form, piles of color-coordinated files sat on the corner, all his pens in the holder. He'd kind of missed Lexie's organization. "Mind if I ask why you're here?" he asked, afraid to wish she was here for him.

"About that." She twisted her hands together nervously. "Have you hired a new assistant?"

"One I've kept? No."

Another small smile edged that too sexy mouth. "Okay, then I'll assume the position is open. And now I'm back, so consider it filled."

This time it was his turn to grin, but the smile slowly faded. "Is it business only?" He asked their familiar refrain, unsure if he could handle her as his personal assistant and nothing more.

They'd been too close. He'd shared too much with her. He'd let himself open up and be himself. And he loved her. So he couldn't just be her boss.

"That depends on you." Before she could elaborate, someone knocked on his office door.

"Shit. I'll get rid of whoever it is," he promised, needing this conversation more than his next breath.

Her eyes opened wide. "No. Umm, you can't. Give

us a minute!" she called out before turning back to Kade. "Listen. I did something and I don't want you to be mad or upset with me."

He narrowed his gaze. "Tell me."

"Well, I know how much you like things orderly and expected. Maybe I didn't think this through as well as I thought, but it's done now, right?"

"You're rambling," he said. "What's going on?"

A loud banging sounded outside his door again. "What?" Kade shouted.

"Your brother is waiting to meet you," Lexie said, ducking around him.

"My brother?" he asked, his chest suddenly hurting and painful. "Brother, as in…"

"Jeffrey, from England," Lexie said, cheeks stained pink. "Just know I did this because I love you. And because I knew it was something that, deep down, you needed." As she spoke, she walked backwards, edging her way to the door and grasping the handle. "And I only invited him after I made sure he felt exactly the same way. He misses you, Kade."

All the moisture drained from his mouth, and words failed him, which was a good thing, because he really didn't want to yell at Lexie for trying to do something nice. Even if that something turned into a disaster. But maybe it wouldn't. And there was that damned *hope* again.

She unlocked the door … and the brother Kade hadn't seen in twenty-three years walked into his office. Kade stared at an older version of the boy he'd known, whose picture he looked at often, despite hiding it behind other photos on his shelf.

"Jeffrey."

"Kade." He extended his hand, Kade shook it, and before he knew it, he was hugging his long-lost sibling. Thanks to Lexie.

AN HOUR LATER, Jeffrey, who Lexie had met at the airport yesterday, left Kade's office, giving her a wink as he strode to the elevator.

She let out a sigh of relief … for the brothers. She still didn't know if Kade was angry with her for meddling. Even if she had his best interest at heart. Not to mention, they'd been mid-serious conversation when Jeffrey had arrived, so things between Lexie and Kade were still up in the air.

When the buzzer rang, she jumped. She picked up the phone. "Yes?"

"In here. Now," Kade said, his voice stern.

Her stomach was doing flips and turns as she entered his office, waiting on the threshold.

"Come in and shut the door." His voice and expression gave no inkling as to his feelings.

She inched in and closed the door behind her. Nervous, she decided to jump right in with her explanation.

"I'm not here for business only," she said, picking up where they'd left off. "When I decided to come back to you, I wanted to make a grand gesture. Something that would prove to you how much I love you."

His eyes flashed a deeper hue at her use of the word love.

She gathered her courage and continued. "The first idea I had was returning as your assistant, because what do you get the man who has everything?" She shrugged. "The one thing he needs the most."

"Someone to make my coffee?" he asked, his eyes twinkling with laughter.

She felt a little better and grinned. "That's part of it. Contacting your brother was the other part. I wanted you to have that connection, and I knew how important it was to you. If I'd gotten any inkling that Jeffrey didn't want that contact too, I'd have put the entire idea to bed."

Kade waited patiently, watching her, his gaze warm, giving her courage.

"As it turns out, Jeffrey had wanted to reach out for years, but your mother convinced him neither you nor your father had any interest in him." She shook her head, hating herself for having to hurt him that way.

To Kade's credit, he didn't even flinch. "She's such a bitch," he muttered.

"I'm sorry." She stepped forward, wanting desperately to touch him, but they weren't *there* … yet.

"I'm over it and her. I swear. Something about meeting you and your immediate acceptance of me… It changed my perspective. It changed me."

She lit up inside at his admission. "You changed things for me too." She drew a deep breath. "You see, a few weeks ago, I took my sister to the Maple Hill Treatment Center upstate. For a long-term stay."

"Come here." He gestured for her to come closer, and she met him by his desk. He grasped her hand in his, and she took comfort from his touch. His thumb caressed her skin, and the heat set her aflame.

"Now go on," he said in a husky tone.

She allowed herself to meet his gaze. "I was sitting alone in the waiting room, and I saw you on television. What you went through, admitting to the date rape accusation, walking away from Blink so you could save Derek and Luke … so Julian wouldn't go after the people you cared about again. You're amazing. And I should have been with you. I *wanted* to be with you."

Understanding settled in his handsome face. "Your sister needed you," he said. "I not only understood that but I respected it."

"And I'm grateful, but don't you see? My sister will *always* need me. Does that mean I don't get a life? Does it mean I don't get to choose you?"

He blinked, then stilled. "Is that what you're doing? Choosing me?" He squeezed her hand tighter, and she understood what he wasn't saying.

"I am. If you still want me." She managed an uncertain smile. "I realized too late why you left the morning after we made love. Because you didn't want to force me to choose. Because you've always come out on the wrong side of that in the past."

"You're right," he admitted.

She reached up and cupped his cheeks. "I told my father it's time for him to step up and be Kendall's parent. That I'm entitled to my own life. I love my sister, and I will always be there for her. But I can't clean up her messes anymore. She has to get there on her own or with the support of my father. When I can help her, I will, but you're my priority, Kade. Does that make me selfish, wanting my own life?" She drew a deep breath and met his gaze. "Wanting you?"

He shook his head, squeezing her wrists and bringing her hands down in front of them. "No, you are not selfish. And I don't ever want you to have to choose between me and your family. You needed me to walk away, to let you cope the way you always had before, so I did. I'll always give you what you need."

"Oh, Kade. I need you. I want you. *I love you.*" She blinked, her eyes watery. "But the one thing I don't want is for you to leave me ever again."

The next thing she knew, she was in his arms, her legs wrapped around his waist, her lips on his, kissing him without coming up for air.

She'd missed him so much.

Kade tugged on Lexie's hair, tilting her head back and drinking his fill of the woman he never thought he'd have in his arms again. Desire swept over him, along with a longing that was soul deep and all consuming.

He backed her against the wall and cushioned his hips between hers. His cock was hard and insistent against her pussy, his brain a haze of want and need. He wasn't focused on anything other than getting inside Lexie again, and considering this was his private office, there was nothing stopping him. He was about to make was a shitty rainy day a spectacular one.

"I mean it, Kade. I love you," she said.

He'd never get tired of hearing those words. As a matter of fact... "I want to hear you say it while I'm balls deep inside you." He pressed a kiss to her nose, her cheeks, her lips.

He needed to hear her say it when they were as physically close as they could be. He'd lose himself in her warm, always willing body and bury the last shred of feeling not quite good enough, once and for all.

Her gaze never leaving his, she unzipped her skirt and let it fall to the floor, then slid her panties off too. Those he shoved in the back pocket of his jeans. She stood before him in sexy heels, her shirt barely covering her sex, legs parted, waiting just for him.

He expelled a harsh breath, then got to work on his belt buckle, dropping his jeans along with his briefs, kicking both aside. He said a prayer of thanks the windows in his office that overlooked the city were the only ones he had to worry about. Nobody in the office could see the perfection that was Lexie, and his alone.

"Come here." With a smile, she stepped toward him. He lifted her into his arms and carried her over to his desk, placing her on the cool aluminum.

"Aren't you glad I cleaned your desk?" she asked.

"So fucking glad," he muttered, stepping between her legs, his solid erection poised and ready, except… "No condom." He hung his head, his entire body protesting reality.

"Kade? Before you, there hadn't been anyone in a long, long time. I had a recent yearly exam. I'm clean." She looked up at him with her gorgeous blue eyes. "And I'm on the pill."

"I'm clean too and I'd never put you at risk."

"Then what are you waiting for?" she asked, leaning back on her elbows, her entire lower body open and ready, exposed to him.

With a groan, he grabbed his cock and rubbed it over her sweet pussy, coating himself with her wetness, nudging himself into her heat.

She whimpered, her body desperately trying to clamp around him. "Now, please."

"Whatever you want," he said, and thrust hard, fast, and deep, groaning as he found heaven inside her tight body. He eased out and pushed back again, burying himself to the hilt.

She pushed herself upward, her eyes on his as their bodies connected in the most intimate way. "I love you, Kade. I don't ever want you to wonder or have to ask for the words. And you'll always come first."

On that sentiment, he released the hold he had on his body, grabbing her hips and pumping into her, grinding their bodies each time they came together. It was hard, it was fast, but it was absolutely perfect. And when he came, the words *I love you* were on his lips.

Epilogue

Three months later…

WHEN IT WAS right, it was right. Kade wanted to bind Lexie to him forever, and she was all too eager to become Mrs. Kaden Barnes. Not that he'd have given her a choice, but she'd accepted his ring, all three carats, and wore it with pride. Although he'd had to convince her that the bus to the office had to go if she wanted to wear her ring. Since she'd moved in with him almost immediately, they shared a car to work every day.

Because Lexie didn't want to bother her father with a wedding, and her sister was still at the treatment center, she decided she wanted to elope in Las Vegas. Which was why they now stood in a private chapel that lacked any tacky Elvis impersonator, and a justice of the peace waited to marry them. They'd flown out with Derek, Luke, and Jeffrey to stand with Kade, and

Tessa and Becky to be Lexie's bridesmaids.

Lexie entered the chapel and took Kade's breath away. She wore a formfitting white gown with beading, a V-neck that had him drooling, and a small tiara atop her head, her long curls falling over her shoulders.

She walked straight to him, her wide smile promising him she was all in.

And all his.

"Is everyone ready?" the judge asked.

"Just one thing first," Kade said, nodding at Derek, who stood by the doors to the chapel.

"You can't get cold feet," Becky warned him.

Lexie narrowed her gaze.

"Not a chance." He glanced at Lexie and grasped her hands, which were cold and clammy in his. "Nervous?" he asked.

"I wasn't … until now."

He merely grinned. "Look."

They all turned toward the doors that Derek opened. Kendall stood by her father's side, wearing a matching bridesmaid's dress to Becky's and Tessa's royal blue ones. Together they walked into the room and headed straight for the bride.

"Oh my God!" Lexie gasped, her beautiful eyes filling with tears. "How?"

"Straight from the institution to Vegas," Kendall joked. "No, seriously. I knew I was being discharged, but I wanted to surprise you." Her twin pulled a shaking Lexie into her arms. "Your soon-to-be husband flew us out on his private jet so we'd be here on time."

"I wouldn't miss my daughter's wedding," her father said. Implied was a scolding for Lexie's attempt at leaving him out in the first place.

Her father had stepped up and done right by both daughters, as well as his wife. Kade admired him for that, even if he'd come late to the realization that the burden shouldn't be on Lexie.

"I don't know what to say. I'm overwhelmed and so happy." Lexie turned to Kade. "I can't believe you arranged this."

He grasped her hands and pulled her over to the corner for a minute alone. "I'd do anything for you. You have to know that. This was just my way of giving you back your family. The same way you returned mine to me."

His brother, a businessman in the import-export business, had moved to the United States to get to know his father and brother. He and Kade had fallen into the same old rhythm, as if no time had passed, and he had Lexie to thank.

She looked up at him. "I adore you, Kaden Barnes."

"And I love you with all my heart, Lexie Parker."

He leaned in and kissed her glossed lips.

"Now let's go get married so you can take my name already."

She rolled her eyes. "Possessive much?" she asked, laughing.

If she only knew. She owned him. And he wouldn't have it any other way.

Preorder the next Billionaire Bad Boy's story (Lucas Monroe and Maxie Sullivan) in
GOING DOWN FAST.

A stand-alone Billionaire Bad Boys novel.

Billionaire Bad Boys: Rich, Powerful and sexy as hell.

Lucas Monroe dropped out of college only to become a multi-billionaire and tech world God. He can have any woman he desires in his bed, but the only woman he's ever wanted is off limits and always has been. When Maxie Sullivan finds herself in dire straights, the only man she can turn to is the one she's always secretly loved: her childhood best friend.

Can they trust their hearts and make a future, or will their complicated pasts stand in the way?

This bad boy is going down fast …

And going down fast has never felt so right.

Thank you for reading **GOING DOWN EASY**. I would appreciate it if you would help others enjoy this book too. Please recommend to others and leave a review.

Meet the Dares!
Dare to Love – Book 1 Dare to Love Series – (Ian Dare)

Keep up with Carly and her upcoming books:

Website:
www.carlyphillips.com

Sign up for Carly's Newsletter:
www.carlyphillips.com/newsletter-sign-up

Carly on Facebook:
www.facebook.com/CarlyPhillipsFanPage

Carly on Twitter:
www.twitter.com/carlyphillips

Hang out at Carly's Corner! (Hot guys & giveaways!)
smarturl.it/CarlysCornerFB

CARLY'S MONTHLY CONTEST!

Visit: www.carlyphillips.com/newsletter-sign-up and enter for a chance to win the prize of the month! You'll also automatically be added to her newsletter list so you can keep up on the newest releases!

Dare to Love Series Reading Order:

Book 1: Dare to Love (Ian & Riley)

Book 2: Dare to Desire (Alex & Madison)

Book 3: Dare to Touch (Olivia & Dylan)

Book 4: Dare to Hold (Scott & Meg)

Book 5: Dare to Rock (Avery & Grey)

Book 6: Dare to Take (Tyler & Ella)

*each book can stand alone for your reading enjoyment

DARE NY Series (NY Dare Cousins) Reading Order:

Book 1: Dare to Surrender (Gabe & Isabelle)

Book 2: Dare to Submit (Decklan & Amanda)

Book 3: Dare to Seduce (Max & Lucy)

*The NY books are more erotic/hotter books

Read on for an excerpt of **Dare to Love**,
Ian and Riley's story.

Dare to Love

Excerpt

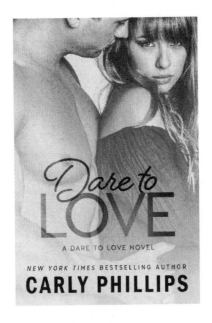

Dare to
LOVE

A DARE TO LOVE NOVEL

NEW YORK TIMES BESTSELLING AUTHOR
CARLY PHILLIPS

Chapter One

ONCE A YEAR, the Dare siblings gathered at the Club Meridian Ballroom in South Florida to celebrate the birthday of the father many of them despised. Ian Dare raised his glass filled with Glenlivet and took a sip, letting the slow burn of fine scotch work its way down his throat and into his system. He'd need another before he fully relaxed.

"Hi, big brother." His sister Olivia strode up to him and nudged him with her elbow.

"Watch the drink," he said, wrapping his free arm around her shoulders for an affectionate hug. "Hi, Olivia."

She returned the gesture with a quick kiss on his cheek. "It's nice of you to be here."

He shrugged. "I'm here for Avery and for you. Although why you two forgave him—"

"Uh-uh. Not here." She wagged a finger in front of

his face. "If I have to put on a dress, we're going to act civilized."

Ian stepped back and took in his twenty-four-year-old sister for the first time. Wearing a gold gown, her dark hair up in a chic twist, it was hard to believe she was the same bane of his existence who'd chased after him and his friends until they relented and let her play ball with them.

"You look gorgeous," he said to her.

She grinned. "You have to say that."

"I don't. And I mean it. I'll have to beat men off with sticks when they see you." The thought darkened his mood.

"You do and I'll have your housekeeper short-sheet your bed! Again, there should be perks to getting dressed like this, and getting laid should be one of them."

"I'll pretend I didn't hear that," he muttered and took another sip of his drink.

"You not only promised to come tonight, you swore you'd behave."

Ian scowled. "Good behavior ought to be optional considering the way he flaunts his assets," he said with a nod toward where Robert Dare held court.

Around him sat his second wife of nine years, Savannah Dare, and their daughter, Sienna, along with their nearest and dearest country club friends. Missing were their other two sons, but they'd show up soon.

Olivia placed a hand on his shoulder. "He loves her, you know. And Mom's made her peace."

"Mom had no choice once she found out about *her*."

Robert Dare had met the much younger Savannah Sheppard and, to hear him tell it, fallen instantly in love. She was now the mother of his three other children, the oldest of whom was twenty-five. Ian had just turned thirty. Anyone could do the math and come up with two families at the same time. The man was beyond fertile, that was for damned sure.

At the reminder, Ian finished his drink and placed the tumbler on a passing server's tray. "I showed my face. I'm out of here." He started for the exit.

"Ian, hold on," his sister said, frustration in her tone.

"What? Do you want me to wait until they sing 'Happy Birthday'? No thanks. I'm leaving."

Before they could continue the discussion, their half brother Alex strode through the double entrance with a spectacular-looking woman holding tightly to his arm, and Ian's plans changed.

Because of *her*.

Some people had presence; others merely wished they possessed that magic something. In her bold, red dress and fuck-me heels, she owned the room. And he wanted to own her. Petite and curvy, with long, chocolate-brown hair that fell down her back in wild curls, she was the antithesis of every too-thin female he'd dated and kept at arm's length. But she was with his half brother, which meant he had to steer clear.

"I thought you were leaving," Olivia said from beside him.

"I am." He should. If he could tear his gaze away from *her*.

"If you wait for Tyler and Scott, you might just relax enough to have fun," she said of their brothers. "Come on, please?" Olivia used the pleading tone he never could resist.

"Yeah, please, Ian? Come on," his sister Avery said, joining them, looking equally mature in a silver gown that showed way too much cleavage. At twenty-two, she was similar in coloring and looks to Olivia, and he wasn't any more ready to think of her as a grown-up—never mind letting other men ogle her—than he was with her sister.

Ian set his jaw, amazed these two hadn't been the death of him yet.

"So what am I begging him to do?" Avery asked Olivia.

Olivia grinned. "I want him to stay and hang out for a while. Having fun is probably out of the question, but I'm trying to persuade him to let loose."

"Brat," he muttered, unable to hold back a smile at Olivia's persistence.

He stole another glance at his lady in red. He could no more leave than he could approach her, he thought, frustrated because he was a man of action, and right now, he could do nothing but watch her.

"Well?" Olivia asked.

He forced his gaze to his sister and smiled. "Because you two asked so nicely, I'll stay." But his attention remained on the woman now dancing and laughing with his half brother.

RILEY TAYLOR FELT his eyes on her from the moment she entered the elegantly decorated ballroom on the arm of another man. As it was, her heels made it difficult enough to maneuver gracefully. Knowing a devastatingly sexy man watched her every move only made not falling on her ass even more of a challenge.

Alex Dare, her best friend, was oblivious. Being the star quarterback of the Tampa Breakers meant he was used to stares and attention. Riley wasn't. And since this was his father's birthday bash, he knew everyone here. She didn't.

She definitely didn't know *him*. She'd managed to avoid this annual party in the past with a legitimate work excuse one year, the flu another, but this year,

Alex knew she was down in the dumps due to job problems, and he'd insisted she come along and have a good time.

While Alex danced with his mother then sisters, she headed for the bar and asked the bartender for a glass of ice water. She took a sip and turned to go find a seat, someplace where she could get off her feet and slip free of her offending heels.

She'd barely taken half a step when she bumped into a hard, suit-clad body. The accompanying jolt sent her water spilling from the top of her glass and into her cleavage. The chill startled her as much as the liquid that dripped down her chest.

"Oh!" She teetered on her stilettos, and big, warm hands grasped her shoulders, steadying her.

She gathered herself and looked up into the face of the man she'd been covertly watching. "You," she said on a breathy whisper.

His eyes, a steely gray with a hint of blue in the depths, sparkled in amusement and something more. "Glad you noticed me too."

She blinked, mortified, no words rushing into her brain to save her. She was too busy taking him in. Dark brown hair stylishly cut, cheekbones perfectly carved, and a strong jaw completed the package. And the most intense heat emanated from his touch as he held on to her arms. His big hands made her feel small, not an easy feat when she was always conscious of her too-full curves.

She breathed in deeply and was treated to a masculine, woodsy scent that turned her insides to pure mush. Full-scale awareness rocked her to her core. This man hit all her right buttons.

"Are you all right?" he asked.

"I'm fine." Or she would be if he'd release her so she could think. Instead of telling him so, she continued to stare into his handsome face.

"You certainly are," he murmured.

A heated flush rushed to her cheeks at the compliment, and a delicious warmth invaded her system.

"I'm sorry about the spill," he said.

At least she hoped he was oblivious to her ridiculous attraction to him.

"You're wet." He released her and reached for a napkin from the bar.

Yes, she was. In wholly inappropriate ways considering they'd barely met. Desire pulsed through her veins. Oh my God, what was it about this man that caused reactions in her body another man would have to work overtime to achieve?

He pressed the thin paper napkin against her chest and neck. He didn't linger, didn't stroke her anywhere he shouldn't, but she could swear she felt the heat of his fingertips against her skin. Between his heady scent and his deliberate touch, her nerves felt raw and exposed. Her breasts swelled, her nipples peaked, and she shivered, her body tightening in places she'd long thought dormant. If he noticed, he was too much of a gentleman to say.

No man had ever awakened her senses this way before. Sometimes she wondered if that was a deliberate choice on her part. Obviously not, she thought and forced herself to step back, away from his potent aura.

He crinkled the napkin and placed the paper onto the bar.

"Thank you," she said.

"My pleasure." The word, laced with sexual innuendo, rolled off his tongue, and his eyes darkened to a deep indigo, an indication that this crazy attraction she experienced wasn't one-sided.

"Maybe now we can move on to introductions. I'm Ian Dare," he said.

She swallowed hard, disappointment rushing through her as she realized, for all her awareness of him, he was the one man at this party she ought to stay away from. "Alex's brother."

"Half brother," he bit out.

"Yes." She understood his pointed correction. Alex wouldn't want any more of a connection to Ian than Ian did to Alex.

"You have your father's eyes," she couldn't help

but note.

His expression changed, going from warm to cold in an instant. "I hope that's the only thing you think that bastard and I have in common."

Riley raised her eyebrows at the bitter tone. Okay, she understood he had his reasons, but she was a stranger.

Ian shrugged, his broad shoulders rolling beneath his tailored, dark suit. "What can I say? Only a bastard would live two separate lives with two separate families at the same time."

"You do lay it out there," she murmured.

His eyes glittered like silver ice. "It's not like everyone here doesn't know it."

Though she ought to change the subject, he'd been open, so she decided to ask what was on her mind. "If you're still so angry with him, why come for his birthday?"

"Because my sisters asked me to," he said, his tone turning warm and indulgent.

A hint of an easier expression changed his face from hard and unyielding to devastatingly sexy once more.

"Avery and Olivia are much more forgiving than me," he explained.

She smiled at his obvious affection for his siblings. As an only child, she envied them a caring, older brother. At least she'd had Alex, she thought and glanced around looking for the man who'd brought her here. She found him on the dance floor, still with his mother, and relaxed.

"Back to introductions," Ian said. "You know my name; now it's your turn."

"Riley Taylor."

"Alex's girlfriend," he said with disappointment. "I saw you two walk in."

That's what he thought? "No, we're friends. More like brother and sister than anything else."

His eyes lit up, and she caught a glimpse of yet another expression—pleasantly surprised. "That's the best news I've heard all night," he said in a deep, compelling tone, his hot gaze never leaving hers.

At a loss for words, Riley remained silent.

"So, Ms. Riley Taylor, where were you off to in such a hurry?" he asked.

"I wanted to rest my feet," she admitted.

He glanced down at her legs, taking in her red pumps. "Ahh. Well, I have just the place."

Before she could argue—and if she'd realized he'd planned to drag her off alone, she might have—Ian grasped her arm and guided her to the exit at the far side of the room.

"Ian—"

"Shh. You'll thank me later. I promise." He

pushed open the door, and they stepped out onto a deck that wasn't in use this evening.

Sticky, night air surrounded them, but being a Floridian, she was used to it, and obviously so was he. His arm still cupping her elbow, he led her to a small love seat and gestured for her to sit.

She sensed he was a man who often got his way, and though she'd never found that trait attractive before, on him, it worked. She settled into the soft cushions. He did the same, leaving no space between them, and she liked the feel of his hard body aligned with hers. Her heart beat hard in her chest, excitement and arousal pounding away inside her.

Around them, it was dark, the only light coming from sconces on the nearby building.

"Put your feet up." He pointed to the table in front of them.

"Bossy," she murmured.

Ian grinned. He was and was damned proud of it. "You're the one who said your feet hurt," he reminded her.

"True." She shot him a sheepish look that was nothing short of adorable.

The reverberation in her throat went straight to Ian's cock, and he shifted in his seat, pure sexual desire now pumping through his veins.

He'd been pissed off and bored at his father's ridiculous birthday gala. Even his sisters had barely been able to coax a smile from him. Then *she'd* walked into the room.

Because she was with his half brother, Ian hadn't planned on approaching her, but the minute he'd caught sight of her alone at the bar, he'd gone after her, compelled by a force beyond his understanding. Finding out she and Alex were just friends had made his night because she'd provide a perfect distraction to the pain that followed him whenever his father's other family was near.

"Shoes?" he reminded her.

She dipped her head and slipped off her heels, moaning in obvious relief.

"That sound makes me think of other things," he said, capturing her gaze.

"Such as?" She unconsciously swayed closer, and he suppressed a grin.

"Sex. With you."

"Oh." Her lips parted with the word, and Ian couldn't tear his gaze away from her lush, red-painted mouth.

A mouth he could envision many uses for, none of them tame.

"Is this how you charm all your women?" she asked. "Because I'm not sure it's working." A teasing smile lifted her lips, contradicting her words.

He had her, all right, as much as she had him.

He kept his gaze on her face, but he wasn't a complete gentleman and couldn't resist brushing his hand over her tight nipples showing through the fabric of her dress.

Her eyes widened in surprise at the same time a soft moan escaped, sealing her fate. He slid one arm across the love seat until his fingers hit her mass of curls, and he wrapped his hand in the thick strands. Then, tugging her close, he sealed his mouth over hers. She opened for him immediately. The first taste was a mere preview, not nearly enough, and he deepened the kiss, taking more.

Sweet, hot, and her tongue tangled with his. He gripped her hair harder, wanting still more. She was like all his favorite vices in one delectable package. Best of all, she kissed him back, every inch a willing, giving partner.

He was a man who dominated and took, but from the minute he tasted her, he gave as well. If his brain were clear, he'd have pulled back immediately, but she reached out and gripped his shoulders, curling her fingers through the fabric of his shirt, her nails digging into his skin. Each thrust of his tongue in her mouth mimicked what he really wanted, and his cock hardened even more.

"You've got to be kidding me," his half brother

said, interrupting at the worst possible moment.

He would have taken his time, but Riley jumped, pushing at his chest and backing away from him at the same time.

"Alex!"

"Yeah. The guy who brought you here, remember?"

Ian cursed his brother's interruption as much as he welcomed the reminder that this woman represented everything Ian resented. His half brother's friend. Alex, with whom he had a rivalry that would have done real siblings proud.

The oldest sibling in the *other* family was everything Ian wasn't. Brash, loud, tattoos on his forearms, and he threw a mean football as quarterback of the Tampa Breakers. Ian, meanwhile, was more of a thinker, president of the Breakers' rivals, the Miami Thunder, owned by his father's estranged brother, Ian's uncle.

Riley jumped up, smoothing her dress and rubbing at her swollen lips, doing nothing to ease the tension emanating from her best friend.

Ian took his time standing.

"I see you met my brother," Alex said, his tone tight.

Riley swallowed hard. "We were just—"

"Getting better acquainted," Ian said in a seductive tone meant to taunt Alex and imply just how much better he now knew Riley.

A muscle ticked in the other man's jaw. "Ready to go back inside?" Alex asked her.

Neither one of them would make a scene at this mockery of a family event.

"Yes." She didn't meet Ian's gaze as she walked around him and came up alongside Alex.

"Good because my dad's been asking for you. He said it's been too long since he's seen you," Alex said, taunting Ian back with the mention of the one person sure to piss him off.

Despite knowing better, Ian took the bait. "Go on. We were finished anyway," he said, dismissing Riley as surely as she'd done to him.

Never mind that she was obviously torn between her friend and whatever had just happened between them; she'd chosen Alex. A choice Ian had been through before and come out on the same wrong end.

In what appeared to be a deliberately possessive move, Alex wrapped an arm around her waist and led her back inside. Ian watched, ignoring the twisting pain in his gut at the sight. Which was ridiculous. He didn't have any emotional investment in Riley Taylor. He didn't do emotion, period. He viewed relationships through the lens of his father's adultery, finding it easier to remain on the outside looking in.

Distance was his friend. Sex worked for him. It

was love and commitment he distrusted. So no matter how different that brief moment with Riley had been, that was all it was.

A moment.

One that would never happen again.

RILEY FOLLOWED ALEX onto the dance floor in silence. They hadn't spoken a word to each other since she'd let him lead her away from Ian. She understood his shocked reaction and wanted to soothe his frazzled nerves but didn't know how. Not when her own nerves were so raw from one simple kiss.

Except nothing about Ian was simple, and that kiss left her reeling. From the minute his lips touched hers, everything else around her had ceased to matter. The tug of arousal hit her in the pit of her stomach, in her scalp as his fingers tugged her hair, in the weight of her breasts, between her thighs and, most telling, in her mind. He was a strong man, the kind who knew what he wanted and who liked to get his way. The type of man she usually avoided and for good reason.

But she'd never experienced chemistry so strong before. His pull was so compelling she'd willingly followed him outside regardless of the fact that she knew without a doubt her closest friend in the world would be hurt if she got close to Ian.

"Are you going to talk to me?" Alex asked, breaking into her thoughts.

"I'm not sure what to say."

On the one hand, he didn't have a say in her personal life. She didn't owe him an apology. On the other, he was her everything. The child she'd grown up next door to and the best friend who'd saved her sanity and given her a safe haven from her abusive father.

She was wrong. She knew exactly what to say. "I'm sorry."

He touched his forehead to hers. "I don't know what came over me. I found you two kissing, and I saw red."

"It was just chemistry." She let out a shaky laugh, knowing that term was too benign for what had passed between her and Ian.

"I don't want you to get hurt. The man doesn't do relationships, Ri. He uses women and moves on."

"Umm, Pot/Kettle?" she asked him. Alex moved from woman to woman just as he'd accused his half brother of doing.

He'd even kissed *her* once. Horn dog that he was, he said he'd had to try, but they both agreed there was no spark and their friendship meant way too much to throw away for a quick tumble between the sheets.

Alex frowned. "Maybe so, but that doesn't change

the facts about him. I don't want you to get hurt."

"I won't," she assured him, even as her heart picked up speed when she caught sight of Ian watching them from across the room.

Drink in hand, brooding expression on his face, his stare never wavered.

She curled her hands into the suit fabric covering Alex's shoulders and assured herself she was telling the truth.

"What if he was using you to get to me?"

"Because the man can't be interested in me for me?" she asked, her pride wounded despite the fact that Alex was just trying to protect her.

Alex slowed his steps and leaned back to look into her eyes. "That's not what I meant, and you know it. Any man would be lucky to have you, and I'd never get between you and the right guy." A muscle pulsed in Alex's right temple, a sure sign of tension and stress. "But Ian's not that guy."

She swallowed hard, hating that he just might be right. Riley wasn't into one-night stands. Which was why her body's combustible reaction to Ian Dare confused and confounded her. How far would she have let him go if Alex hadn't interrupted? Much further than she'd like to imagine, and her body responded with a full-out shiver at the thought.

"Now can we forget about him?"

Not likely, she thought, when his gaze burned hotter than his kiss. Somehow she managed to swallow over the lump in her throat and give Alex the answer he sought. "Sure."

Pleased, Alex pulled her back into his arms to continue their slow dance. Around them, other guests, mostly his father's age, moved slowly in time to the music.

"Did I mention how much I appreciate you coming here with me?" Obviously trying to ease the tension between them, he shot her the same charming grin that had women thinking they were special.

Riley knew better. She *was* special to him, and if he ever turned his brand of protectiveness on the right kind of woman and not the groupies he preferred, he might find himself settled and happy one day. Sadly, he didn't seem to be on that path.

She decided to let their disagreement over Ian go. "I believe you've mentioned how wonderful I am a couple of times. But you still owe me one," Riley said. Parties like this weren't her thing.

"It took your mind off your job stress, right?" he asked.

She nodded. "Yes, and let's not even talk about that right now." Monday was soon enough to deal with her new boss.

"You got it. Ready for a break?" he asked.

She nodded. Unable to help herself, she glanced over where she'd seen Ian earlier, but he was gone. The disappointment twisting the pit of her stomach was disproportional to the amount of time she'd known him, and she blamed that kiss.

Her lips still tingled, and if she closed her eyes and ran her tongue over them, she could taste his heady, masculine flavor. Somehow she had to shake him from her thoughts. Alex's reaction to seeing them together meant Riley couldn't allow herself the luxury of indulging in anything more with Ian.

Not even in her thoughts or dreams.

About the Author

Carly Phillips is the *N.Y. Times* and *USA Today* Best-selling Author of over 50 sexy contemporary romance novels featuring hot men, strong women and the emotionally compelling stories her readers have come to expect and love. Carly's career spans over a decade and a half with various New York publishing houses, and she is now an Indie author who runs her own business and loves every exciting minute of her publishing journey. Carly is happily married to her college sweetheart, the mother of two nearly adult daughters and three crazy dogs (two wheaten terriers and one mutant Havanese) who star on her Facebook Fan Page and website. Carly loves social media and is always around to interact with her readers. You can find out more about Carly at www.carlyphillips.com.

CARLY'S BOOKLIST

by Series

Billionaire Bad Boys Reading Order:

Book 1: Going Down Easy

Book 2: Going Down Fast

Book 3: Going Down Hard

Dirty, Sexy Reading Order:

Book 1: Dirty Sexy Saint

Book 2: Dirty Sexy Inked

Book 3: Dirty Sexy Cuffed

Book 4: Dirty Sexy Sinner

Dare to Love Series Reading Order:

Book 1: Dare to Love (Ian & Riley)

Book 2: Dare to Desire (Alex & Madison)

Book 3: Dare to Touch (Olivia & Dylan)

Book 4: Dare to Hold (Scott & Meg)

Book 5: Dare to Rock (Avery & Grey)

Book 6: Dare to Take (Tyler & Ella)

*each book can stand alone for your reading enjoyment

DARE NY Series (NY Dare Cousins) Reading Order:

Book 1: Dare to Surrender (Gabe & Isabelle)

Book 2: Dare to Submit (Decklan & Amanda)

Book 3: Dare to Seduce (Max & Lucy)

*The NY books are more erotic/hotter books

Carly Classics

The Right Choice

Suddenly Love (formerly titled Kismet)

Perfect Partners

Unexpected Chances (formerly titled Midnight Angel)

Worthy of Love (formerly titled Solitary Man)

Carly's Earlier
Traditionally Published Books

Serendipity Series

Serendipity

Destiny

Karma

Serendipity's Finest Series

Perfect Fit

Perfect Fling

Perfect Together

Serendipity Novellas

Fated

Hot Summer Nights (Perfect Stranger)

Bachelor Blog Series

Kiss Me If You Can

Love Me If You Dare

Lucky Series

Lucky Charm

Lucky Streak

Lucky Break

Ty and Hunter Series

Cross My Heart

Sealed with a Kiss

Hot Zone Series

Hot Stuff

Hot Number

Hot Item

Hot Property

Costas Sisters Series

Summer Lovin'

Under the Boardwalk

Chandler Brothers Series

The Bachelor

The Playboy

The Heartbreaker

Stand Alone Titles

Brazen

Seduce Me

Secret Fantasy

87034277R00158

Made in the USA
Lexington, KY
18 April 2018